The chariot switched back and forth violently, shaking Pandora like a rag. She was losing her grip, frantically clutching the floorboards with two fingers and a thumb.

"Pandy!" Iole yelled.

Held fast by Alcie, Iole was just about to reach Pandy's wrist when the horses started a steep descent, throwing the chariot up once more.

"Oh, Gods! Iole!" Pandy cried as the last bit of wood slid out from under her fingertips . . .

. . . and she fell, screaming, to the earth.

MYTHIC MISADVENTURES
BY CAROLYN HENNESY

Pandora Gets Jealous
Pandora Gets Vain
Pandora Gets Lazy
Pandora Gets Heart

PANDORA
Gets Lazy

BOOK III

CAROLYN HENNESY

BLOOMSBURY

NEW YORK BERLIN LONDON

First published in the United States of America in April 2009
by Bloomsbury Books for Young Readers
Paperback edition published in May 2010
www.bloomsburykids.com

For information about permission to reproduce selections from this book, write to
Permissions, Bloomsbury BFYR, 175 Fifth Avenue, New York, New York 10010

The Library of Congress has cataloged the hardcover edition as follows:
Hennesy, Carolyn.
Pandora gets lazy / by Carolyn Hennesy.—1st U.S. ed.
p.   cm.
Summary: On their way to find the third evil, laziness, Pandy and her friends,
Alcie, Iole, and Homer, face many dangers after Pandy falls from Apollo's chariot
and her friends are captured by pirates who intend to sell them into slavery.
ISBN-13: 978-1-59990-198-5 • ISBN-10: 1-59990-198-6 (hardcover)
1. Pandora (Greek mythology)—Juvenile fiction. [1. Pandora (Greek mythology)—
Fiction. 2. Mythology, Greek—Fiction. 3. Gods, Greek—Fiction. 4. Goddesses,
Greek—Fiction. 5. Adventures and adventurers—Fiction.] I. Title.
PZ7.H3917Paq 2009   [Fic]—dc22   2008034855

ISBN-13: 978-1-59990-481-8 (paperback)

Typeset by Westchester Book Composition
Printed in the U.S.A. by Worldcolor Fairfield, Pennsylvania
1 3 5 7 9 10 8 6 4 2

All papers used by Bloomsbury Publishing, Inc., are natural, recyclable products
made from wood grown in well-managed forests. The manufacturing processes
conform to the environmental regulations of the country of origin.

For Donald
Lakh tirikh

CHAPTER ONE
The Chariot of the Sun

It was painfully obvious . . .

Sometime in the last few weeks, Pandy had stopped biting her nails. At some point since she and her friends had begun the quest to find the evils she had mistakenly released into the world, she had unconsciously given up that silly childhood habit.

Pandy knew it now from the way her nails dug into her palms as she clutched the hem of Iole's thin cloak in one hand, her other fist madly wiping away a flow of tears from her eyes. Four tiny red half crescents were burning on each hand, yet she didn't relax her grip. Even when Iole had said that her thin legs were starting to cramp from crouching and that she was going to stand for just a bit, Pandy stayed doubled over and hung on.

Pandy, Alcie, Iole, and Homer had all expected their short trip from Egypt to the Atlas Mountains to be like any other chariot ride, bumpy and jostling. But they were all riding in Apollo's Sun Chariot and the magnificent white steeds were running through the air as smoothly as if they were standing still.

For the last five minutes Pandy, curled into a ball in the very front, had concentrated solely on the fact that seconds before they departed Alexandria, she'd discovered that the goddess Hera had stolen her dog, Dido. Weeping, she had caught only snippets of her friends' chatter as they stood upright around her.

"Excuse me," she'd heard Alcie shout, looking off to the side of the chariot, "but over there, way off in the distance? Uh . . . where is the world?"

"Isn't it exciting?" Iole had answered. "I knew my theory was correct. It's just as I calculated: the earth is round!"

"Yeah, right!" scoffed Homer, turning his gaze from the horizon ahead, his hands tight on the reins.

"Oh, oranges, Iole," said Alcie. "If the world was round, all the oceans and seas would drain off the side. Everybody knows that."

"Doubt me all you like, but if the earth was flat, we'd be able to see it far off into the distance, yet observe how it curves? That's because it's a sphere!"

Pandy took a deep breath and opened her eyes.

"Sphere, schmere—," Alcie began.

"I want to stand!" Pandy interrupted, sniffling up to her friends.

"Thatta girl!" Iole said. "Then you can help me explain to Alcie why the earth has to be round and—"

"Please, just help me up," said Pandy. "Hera and Dido might not be that far away. Maybe I can spot him."

On her feet, she peered over the side of the chariot, careful not to touch the white-hot outer sides as it pulled the sun just a few meters behind them.

"Pandy," Alcie said gently, "Hera's probably back on Olympus by now. I don't think . . . oh . . . oh! . . . Iole, catch her!"

Iole grabbed Pandy's arm as she doubled over in a fresh spasm of grief, almost brushing her cheek against the topside of the chariot.

"Why would she steal Dido?" Pandy wailed. "He's done nothing to her! Even when she appeared to us in Greece, he just hid under the pallet. He didn't try to bite her! He didn't even growl!"

"Look," said Iole, "I will bet you she doesn't harm one hair on his body. There's no way she could kidnap one of us without Zeus finding out that she's meddling with your quest. We'd make too much fuss. But she can hide Dido someplace and Zeus will never know. I'm telling you, Pandy, she did this because she knew you'd react just as you have. You're thrown off track; your concentration on the quest is gone. Stay focused, finish the quest, and you'll get Dido back, I promise."

Pandy looked from Iole to Alcie.

"Promise," Alcie whispered, nodding her head.

"Hey . . . um . . . I kinda have a problem here," Homer said, his arms struggling with the chariot reins. "Handling the horses from back here was, like, fine when you guys were crouched in the front, but now that you're all, like, standing, I . . . uh . . . can't see."

The girls gingerly moved around Homer so he could see. Iole noticed that Alcie gave his stomach a slight hug with one arm, and Homer patted her hand when she slid past him.

Pandy looked over the side of the chariot and almost stumbled again. The landscape underneath was flying by at a speed she almost couldn't comprehend. Her head began to throb painfully, as if dryads with sharp sticks were poking her from the inside, and she thought she might be sick. She shut her eyes against the vision below, thinking of frescoes on building walls back home in Athens and how a good rain on fresh colors would make them run and bleed. That was what the world was like at this moment: a huge, runny painting. As she hid her face, she had an overwhelming urge to pitch herself out of the chariot and drop toward the earth. She felt Iole's hand reaching for her, and Pandy managed to grab her friend's cloak again.

It was only then that she became aware of the sound. A low hum completely surrounding her, like a billion bees swarming around her head, and underneath this, a steady, persistent double throb.

"Do you hear that?" Alcie said.

"I do!" answered Iole.

"What is it?" Homer cried, raising his voice, his eyes searching above and below.

"It sounds like a machine!" Pandy cried, flashing on a theater play she'd seen once in Athens and the strange contraption called the deus ex machina, which lowered an actor, playing a god, to the theater floor.

"No," she thought, "not a machine . . . not with this strange double beat." She'd heard this throbbing before. No, that wasn't right either . . .

She'd felt it.

When she was scared or tired as a little girl and her father had held her head close to his chest as he comforted her or put her to sleep, she'd felt the same throbbing.

It was the sound of a heartbeat.

"It's a pulse!" she cried.

"Apricots!" yelled Alcie. "What creature is that big? And *where* is it?"

But Pandy instinctively knew that this came from no creature—not one that she could ever imagine, anyway. It was the sound of something far more important, as if it were the beating heart of Zeus himself, powering the machinery that kept the world alive. Then she looked at the horizon in front and was jolted out of her contemplation.

"Uh, what's that?" Pandy asked, staring straight ahead.

"What?" asked Alcie.

"That."

"Great Zeus!" Iole's voice was almost lost.

Ahead, but no telling how far, an immense wall of filmy darkness had appeared, like an endless black privacy curtain, stretching from the top of the sky down to where it almost touched the earth. With Apollo's horses flying at such tremendous speed, the wall was almost upon them. The horses began to slow imperceptibly.

"That is, like, so not good," Homer said.

Suddenly, Pandy heard a sound that made her own pulse stop and her heart drop out of her body.

Far, far off to her right, Dido was yelping for her. Somehow he'd managed to escape, Pandy was sure of it, and he was trying to find his way back to her! She turned her gaze from the terrible black wall ahead, searching every centimeter of the sky.

"Dido! It's Dido!" she cried. "He's trying to find us!"

"What are you talking about, Pandy?" shouted Alcie.

Dido's yelp was closer . . . and now he sounded as if he was in pain. Still Apollo's chariot flew through the sky.

"Can't you hear him? He's right there!"

"He can't be, Pandy! It's a trick!" yelled Iole.

"Dido!" she screamed. "Here, boy!"

But these last words were drowned out as they all heard the sound of a high-pitched cackle—Hera laughing over the rush of air.

The horses heard it as well. Terrified, the lead stallion frantically reared up on his hind legs, and the other three horses all pulled up short. Alcie instinctively grabbed on to Homer. The chariot bucked up and down with a quick heave; the sun, trailing behind, threw a shower of sparks into the air. Iole was flung screaming toward the back opening, her ankle caught at the last moment by Alcie.

But Pandora, with only the slightest grip on Iole's cloak, was thrown out of the chariot and high into the air. She dropped like a lead weight, only to catch herself with one hand on the end of the chariot floorboards; dark, old wood, made slippery smooth after eons of bearing the weight of Apollo. Pandy's hand instantly began sliding off the end, her arm coming close to the spot where the old wood joined the white-hot gold of the outside of the chariot. Iole tried to grab her wrist but was thrown to the side as a spark from the sun landed on a horse, searing his flank and causing him to writhe in agony. Again, the chariot switched back and forth violently, shaking Pandora like a rag. She was losing her grip, frantically clutching the floorboards with two fingers and a thumb.

"Pandy!" Iole yelled.

Held fast by Alcie, Iole was just about to reach Pandy's wrist when the horses started a steep descent, throwing the chariot up once more.

"Oh, Gods! Iole!" Pandy cried as the last bit of wood slid out from under her fingertips and she fell, screaming, to the earth.

As she dropped like a rock, the ground rushing up to meet her, she heard two different sounds very clearly before she passed out: Hera, giggling like a happy baby, and her three best friends, their screams combining into one enormous, terrified wail.

CHAPTER TWO
Landing

The throb of the pulse now far behind them, the stallions were racing noses down, parallel with the black wall, on a collision course with the ground. Their legs moving so fast that the wind they created snapped the reins right out of Homer's hands, causing them to lash and flick wildly in the air—deadly whips, one of which grazed him on the forehead.

"Get down!" cried Homer.

Iole was already tangled on top of Alcie when she felt Homer's cloak cover the both of them, blocking out the light as he crouched over them. Sparks from the sun were somehow finding their way into the chariot and were starting to burn little holes in the fabric of the cloak. Iole caught a glimpse of Alcie's face in the darkness, under her curly hair. She was staring straight at Iole, eyes wide, her face perfectly still.

All of a sudden, they were shoved farther back toward

the opening, as if they were being forced to make room for something new in the chariot. Homer gave a loud groan as he was squeezed between Alcie, Iole, and what felt like two large pillars that had materialized out of thin air.

Lifting the cloak from his eyes, Homer's gaze traveled up two immense legs, over the torso, and right up into the eyes of Apollo.

"Whistle?" the god asked calmly.

Homer, realizing the tiny silver whistle was still clutched in his hand, slowly extended his arm. Alcie and Iole pulled the cloak away from their faces and peered up at the Sun God.

"Thank you so much," Apollo said. "And now . . ."

He instantaneously caught both reins and blew the whistle. Immediately the horses slowed and leveled off, maintaining a calmer pace.

For a few seconds, Homer, Alcie, and Iole just looked at one another.

"Oh, come now," Apollo's voice bellowed above them, "stand if you will. There is nothing more to fear."

Cautiously, the three got to their feet. Alcie saw it first. "Tangerines!"

The ground was so close that Iole could have leaned out the back of the chariot and touched it with her fingers. If Apollo had delayed one second more, they would have been dashed to smithereens!

"Cutting it pretty close!" Alcie snapped. Then she immediately slapped her hand over her mouth. "I mean—thank you so, so much!"

"Did you really think I would let anything happen?" Apollo asked. "Not that anything could actually damage the chariot. It's impervious to bumps, scratches, and crashing from great heights."

"Well, that's reassuring—," Iole began.

"Of course, you three would have died a horrible death," Apollo went on, "but the chariot would have been fine. Just wasn't so certain about the horses."

"As Alcie said, O God of Truth, we thank you so much," Iole answered.

"As for you, my fine youth"—Apollo turned to Homer—"nicely done, if I do say so myself. Except for this last little bit where you let them get completely away from you—"

"*Let* them?" Alcie yelped.

Iole kicked her.

Apollo ignored them both, continuing, "—I'd say it was a first-rate job. A thrill, yes? One for the books?"

"Yes, great Apollo," Homer said.

"Here, you took them up, you bring them down," Apollo said, offering the reins back to Homer.

"Uh . . ." Homer balked.

"There's nothing like it, my boy. Feeling the touch-down of the wheels upon the earth, feeling the steeds come to rest. And this chance will not pass your way again."

Homer took the reins and the whistle and, pulling back ever so slightly, brought the mighty chariot down with not a bump, skip, or jostle, on a small stretch of beach between the filmy black wall running far away to the west and the Mediterranean Sea to the northeast. Off in the distance, perhaps twenty or so kilometers, they could see another landmass rising out of the water.

"Bravo!" Apollo cried. "Worthy of me. Almost. All right, everyone out!"

At once, they heard the sizzle and crackle as the sun, now on the ground, began turning the earth around it to molten lava.

Homer practically threw Alcie out of the chariot and clear of the lava pool and he was just about to toss Iole when she hesitated and turned to Apollo.

"Please, sir. You are the God of Truth. I'm begging you . . . Where is Pandy—Pandora?"

"I'd hurry, if I were you," Apollo said with a smile.

Leaping out of the chariot after Iole, Homer raced with the others toward the ocean as the lava pool began to widen. Alcie turned back to Apollo just as he was about to blow his whistle.

"Please—please! What happened to Pandy? Did she survive the . . . ?"

"I wouldn't worry about that at the moment. In

about three minutes, you'll have a more immediate and serious problem to deal with. You might want to prepare. Run away, or something. I don't know what you humans do in a case like this. Farewell!"

With that, he snapped the reins and blew the whistle and the golden chariot lifted effortlessly into the air, carrying the sun back into the heavens. The circle of molten earth quickly began to slow its widening, the outer edges turning from glowing red to a toasted dark brown.

"They just leave us!" Alcie said, rushing back to the others. "Dolphins. Gods. They just toss off mysterious things that make us go 'Huh?' and 'What?' and then they're gone! We don't even know where we are. What's coming in three minutes?"

"Two and a half now," said Iole.

"Iole, we've got to find Pandy!" Alcie's voice was rising into a shriek.

"I know and we will, but Apollo himself just gave us a warning. We've got to pay attention! We can't do anything without her, and we'll be no good to her if we're dead. Just calm down a little."

"*You* be calm when *your* best friend is probably—"

"I don't know what happened to *my* best friend—"

"Both of you stop. Gods, is this what girls do? You're, like, *all* best friends, so knock it off, okay? Let's go," said Homer, moving away to the west.

"Why that way?" Iole asked defiantly.

"Because I'm guessing we're on the African continent, probably Mauretania, and those four or five peaks to our left are part of the Pillars of Hercules. It's one big rock Hercules supposedly split into two. There's one pillar across the strait in Espania and one here, and even if I could climb them, you two probably couldn't. There are smaller hills and dunes this way where we can hide from whatever or whoever. There's a huge black wall in front of us and there's, like, the biggest ship I've ever seen about two hundred meters out in the water."

"Oh," Iole said, looking out to sea, "that's why."

"Nice job, Homie," Alcie said, very matter-of-factly, as she and Iole hurried to keep pace as the three of them skirted the huge lava pool.

"Homie?" Iole's voice was up about an octave. "Who's *Homie*?"

"Shhhhh!" Homer whispered as he started up the side of a large dune. Suddenly he stopped and looked back at them.

"Iole, spread your cloak out to your sides."

Iole cocked her head to one side, looked at her cloak, looked at the ground—then flung her arms wide.

Alcie clenched her hands.

"I so hate it when I don't know what's going on!"

"My cloak is the closest to the color of the sand. If

they're looking from the ship, they'll have a harder time seeing us if we hide under it. Come on!"

The three moved slowly up the dune, with Alcie clinging tightly to Iole so most of Iole's cloak could be used to shield Homer's substantial mass. They were almost to the crest, their heads bent low, their eyes on the ground, and their voices stilled.

Alcie dared to break the silence.

"Well," she whispered, "it's been over three minutes and nothing. I think we're probably safe—"

An enormous array of spearheads, some black with dried blood, some still red and shiny, were suddenly thrust under their noses, the tips pointing directly toward their hearts.

CHAPTER THREE
Wake Up

The first thing Pandy thought, even though she was still in that first dozy stage of waking up, was that she'd had quite enough of falling from great heights for the time being, thank you very much. Dropping through the desert floor into the Chamber of Despair in Egypt, terrified into thinking she was plummeting to her death when she woke on Olympus . . . it was all just too much. And now this: flung out of Apollo's chariot thousands of kilometers above the earth, her friends screaming after her. At least, she now thought, she'd had the good sense to pass out before she'd been smashed to pieces.

But if she'd been broken into five million bits, why was she able to wiggle her toes? And her fingers? And why was she able to feel prickles all over her body?

Opening her eyes, she saw dark, feathery objects directly overhead, and beyond that, the clear, deep blue sky. She slowly realized she was staring at the topmost branches of an enormous pine tree and she was lying, cradled actually, in one of its larger boughs. Pandy turned her head slightly and peered through the clusters of pine needles and cones. The ground was at least one hundred meters below.

"Oh, great," she thought, "another fall."

But before she had a chance to see if there might be a way to climb down, the branch began rolling slowly to her left. Panic took over . . . as the branch was obviously dumping her . . . and Pandy began clawing frantically at needles, pinecones, and short twigs—anything! Everything she grabbed at moved itself swiftly out of her reach except for two new shoots of tiny needles. Desperately, Pandy grasped these with all her strength so that when the branch was almost completely overturned, she was simply hanging in midair underneath. Suddenly the branch lifted up and gave a gentle shake, weakening Pandy's grip and jiggling her loose. With a shriek she dropped off of the branch . . .

And onto the branch below.

The new branch bounced for a bit with her added weight, settled for a moment, and then rolled slowly to the left. Instinctively, Pandy grabbed at anything within reach, but this time, the needles pricked her fingers and the larger twigs rapped her knuckles, batting her hand away. Astonished, she slid awkwardly off the new branch and onto the one below that.

Rolling branch after branch in a descending spiral, the giant tree lowered her to the ground. Toward the end Pandy, who had completely subdued her instinct to grab hold of anything, was experimenting with different sliding and dropping positions: curled up like a ball (her water-skin and carrying pouch in her arms), lying flat with her arms folded in front like a mummy, or holding her arms to her sides and rolling like the chicken legs Sabina would fry in olive oil back home. She had almost perfected the best move (lying on her side, legs tucked, arms folded, which meant she was getting almost no needles sticking to her) when she was deposited, very delicately, on the ground. She stood immediately and faced the pine, aware that, although she was in a part of the world she knew nothing about, it could easily be inhabited by dryads or that the tree could be a conscious or enchanted thing.

"Thank you," she said loudly.

There was only the rustling of the wind in the branches for an answer.

Pandy turned to survey her surroundings. She was on top of a large, rocky rise ringed by mountains and hills on all sides; she could see a single road winding its way around the base of the hills off in the distance. Although she was standing in the middle of a flat, barren clearing between several trees, when she inched her way over to the edge she was stunned to see a sharp drop of nearly two hundred meters. It wasn't quite straight down, but it was severe enough that Pandy knew she could never attempt the descent. Walking around the edge of what was, apparently, a large flat spire of rock, she could see only scrubby, uninviting brush dotted with an occasional olive tree clinging desperately to the side. There was no road or walking path off the spire: no way down . . . period. And there were no signs of life in any direction: no smoke from a cooking fire, no dust from a chariot on the road winding through the mountains, no temple pillar rising into the sky. What she did notice, however, to her left, was a darkening of the sky, and it became darker the farther west she looked. She realized it was the same filmy black wall they'd seen while riding the Sun Chariot. But other than that, she saw nothing to get to and, more importantly, no way to get there.

Where were Alcie, Iole, and Homer? Had they survived the chariot ride? Were they hurt? Alive? If so, they were probably frantic with worry.

Without warning, something hit her on top of her head. Instinctively she reached up, but whatever it was had fallen to the ground. She continued to scan the hill for a way down to the road. Something else hit her head, this time with a little more force. She looked into the sky. Nothing. Staring at the ground she saw two little pine nuts lying side by side in the dark brown earth. Another hit her on top of her head and fell alongside the other two.

"I *said* thank you!" she cried to the pine tree. "Was I supposed to do something . . . ?"

Before she'd even finished her question, she watched in amazement as every branch on the tree began to quiver. Suddenly, Pandy was caught in a downpour of fresh white pine nuts. They rained so hard and so fast that Pandy could only throw her arms over her head for protection. A few seconds later, when the deluge stopped, she was rooted where she stood, knee-deep in a huge mound of nuts. As she tried to step out, every nut on the ground instantly scurried away to form another large pile.

Pandy, unsure of what to do, kept looking from the tree to the pile and back again.

"Okaaay," she finally said.

Immediately, the pile began to re-form itself. Nuts moving alone or in little groups, left, right, up, and down, stacking themselves on top of each other, forming little shapes that would unite with other little shapes, some balancing precariously on others, until they formed a single recognizable word:

OKAY!

Then the nuts re-formed again, this time faster, into a sentence.

HOW ARE YOU?

"Fine," Pandy whispered in awe.

EXCELLENT! I WAS WORRIED! the nuts spelled out.

"You were . . . Who . . . ?"

. . . IS THIS?

"Uh-huh."

THREE GUESSES!

"Um . . . Hermes? *Ow!*" She'd named the only god she'd spoken with who had a sense of humor, when suddenly a pinecone hit her squarely on top of her head. She looked up to see a large gray squirrel sitting on a high branch with a mound of pinecones at his side.

SO VERY, VERY WRONG!

"Sorry. Uh . . ."

WANT A CLUE?

"Yeah, I mean, yes, thank you. I mean, please."

I'M *CRUSHED* THAT YOU CAN'T GUESS. YOU HAVE TWO MORE TRIES!

There were so many words that there weren't enough nuts to finish the exclamation point, so the sentences had to wait until the tree shook a few more loose, giving Pandy time to think. Crushed? Wheat was crushed for flour and olives for oil . . . both of which came from the earth.

"Demeter?" she said timidly.

Bonk! Another enormous pinecone bounced off her skull.

"*Ow!*" she cried louder, glaring at the squirrel, whose little claws were already clutching another cone.

LAST CLUE . . . READY?

"I guess . . . ," Pandy mumbled.

PLEASE DON'T WINE IF YOU DON'T GUESS RIGHT! spelled the nuts.

"I won't whine . . ." She suddenly noticed something wrong. "Wine" for "whine"? "Crushed"? Crushed grapes make wine!

"Dionysus?" she said, immediately covering her head with her arms.

CORRECT! spelled the pine nuts in huge letters. Then the nuts lay horizontal for a second, then back to vertical, then alternating between the two . . . making it look like the word was flashing. After a few seconds, the nuts quickly formed the legs, torso, arms, and head of a huge man. Suddenly the eyelids popped open and two bluish green eyeballs stared at Pandy as the figure began to move.

"Dionysus?" Pandy asked.

"Oh, sorry . . . hang on," the god said through his pine-nut mouth. A handful of nuts left the hem of his nut-toga and re-formed as a ring of grape leaves circling his head. Others formed a wine goblet in his right hand.

"There we go!" he laughed. "Recognize me now?"

"Yes, sir."

"Good girl! Very proud," he said, slurring his words just the tiniest bit as he skipped and danced around the clearing, sending the occasional stray pine nut flying. "No time to lose, however. You're heading into dangerous territory, sweet maiden. Had I known, when I put Laziness in the box lo those eons ago, where it would settle if it was ever released, well, I would have thought twice, I can tell you. Here's a clue, very general, mind you: do you like hair? I love mine. So dark and curly. But the form of Laziness . . ."

He shuddered where he stood, all the little nuts jiggling at once.

". . . it's *disgusting*. Icky. All right, enough of that. No more clues. Now, you must find your way into the High Atlas Mountains up to the tallest peak, called Jbel Toubkal, and isn't *that* the funniest name you've ever heard! I swear on my own toenails, these Libyans have the funniest names for things. Say it with me: *Jbel Toooobkaaal!* Oh, I can't stand it!"

But Pandy's memory had been activated. Where had she heard that strange name before? Someone else used to make a joke out of it as well . . . but who?

Dionysus had begun to laugh so hard that he swallowed a few nuts from his own tongue and began to choke. When he couldn't stop, he frantically motioned behind him and then beckoned to Pandy, who rushed over and began whacking his nut-back as hard as she could. Finally, Dionysus coughed up a few stray nuts and caught his breath. As he stared up into the enormous pine, avoiding Pandy's eyes, his voice took on a deeply serious—and sober—tone.

"Let's just keep the fact that I nearly choked on myself our little secret, yes?"

"Absolutely," she agreed.

"And continuing. Right now you're in the Middle Atlas. It was as far as I could let the wind carry you when you fell, without drawing attention . . . but it's only a short two-week walk. Down first, then a whole lotta up. And I'll try to arrange a few signposts . . . keep you on the straight and dangerously narrow." He paused, putting a nut-hand on a nearby tree.

"But I don't see any way down from here," Pandy began. "It's almost a straight drop . . . *Ow!*"

Three pinecones conked her head in rapid succession.

"You humans have absolutely no faith!" said Dionysus. "That's become the major topic of conversation over ambrosia on Olympus: humans losing their faith. So depressing. Right, then, so you know where you have to go. Your friends will most likely show up if they're not killed, and then you can capture this horrible thing and I can stop worrying! About my little contribution, at least. Let someone else take over. I'm simply exhausted!"

And with that, every pine nut dropped to the ground, leaving only two blinking bluish green eyeballs.

"Ready?" she heard Dionysus's voice on the wind.

"Yes, sir," Pandy said.

Instantaneously, the eyeballs disappeared and the

pine nuts re-formed themselves into a large, shallow cup shaped exactly like the top of a fancy wine goblet, only it was about two meters in diameter and perhaps four centimeters thick.

Not knowing what to do, Pandy just stood where she was. Was the god going to fill it with wine? He couldn't possibly want her to drink—

Then a few stray nuts formed the words GET IN! as another pinecone crashed right into her skull.

"You wouldn't be so brave if you were down here!" she shouted at the squirrel. In a flash the squirrel scampered down the tree trunk until he was level with Pandy, then he lobbed a cone right into her forehead, chattering delightedly.

"Why I . . . ," Pandy sputtered.

PLAY WITH THE ANIMALS LATER, PANDORA! spelled the nuts.

Scowling at the squirrel, she climbed into the pine-nut cup, surprised to find how sturdy it was. Immediately the cup began moving toward the edge of the clearing, forcing Pandy to sit down. Realizing it was heading over the edge, she gripped the rim of the cup with all her might.

"Waaahhhh!"

She couldn't stop herself from screaming as the cup sailed down the steep descent, bumping, pitching, and lurching as it picked up greater and greater speed. Pandy felt every crash into each shrub, every collision with the larger rocks, and had to duck several times as the cup flew under low-hanging olive branches.

"It's Dionysus. He likes me. He's told me where to go. It's Dionysus. He likes me. He's told me where to go," she chanted over and over to herself.

The cup careened into a thick, nasty-looking cluster of yellowish shrubs, veered slightly left, then sailed off a rocky outcrop as Pandy became airborne for almost ten seconds.

"But he liiiiikes meeeee," she screamed, just as the cup rose up underneath her again.

With the speed of one of Zeus's lightning bolts, the cup headed for the bottom of the hill, straight on a crash course with a cluster of enormous boulders. Feeling only fairly certain that she wasn't going to be killed, Pandy gritted her teeth and held her breath. The boulders were only seconds away. She closed her eyes as tightly as she could; if, this time, she really was going to be dashed to bits, she didn't want to see it coming.

But with her eyes still closed, Pandy missed seeing the two small boys emerge from behind one especially large boulder.

For their part, watching a screaming girl in a flying white object bearing straight for them, the boys, all alone and nearly delirious with hunger, both thought separately that they had finally died, and they prayed that this was a very loud but hopefully gentle spirit coming to reunite them with the spirits of their family.

Centimeters before crashing, the cup came to a stop so fast that the bottom skidded over some smooth, flat rocks, creating enormous friction and heat, and Pandy smelled the delicious aroma of roasted pine nuts.

Opening her eyes, Pandy stared straight up at the boulder and let out a colossal sigh of relief.

Then, as movement caught her eye, she turned and gaped at two little boys standing very close, both of whom threw their hands up in the air and immediately fell to their knees.

CHAPTER FOUR

Captive

There were so many spears, they couldn't count them all. But the spears themselves were very short, almost tiny, as were the creatures holding them.

Alcie, Iole, and Homer were each alternating between fear, repulsion, and tremendous, Pandy-esque curiosity.

Their attackers resembled little men, or boys, with wrinkled blackish skin mottled with cracked patches of red, as if they'd been burned by something, healed, then burned again. And their bodies were horribly distorted; necks seemed to have been jammed between shoulder blades, backs were hunched over and caved in, and spines were twisted at horrible angles.

"It's as if these—*things*—were broken, then shrunk, then reset—by a blind man," Iole thought.

But no one had time to think anything else, as more tiny creatures that had circled around behind began prodding them up onto the crest of the dune. They were thrown to the ground (ten creatures jabbed Homer in his legs with their spears to get him to comply); individually, their hands and feet were bound in tight shackles. Alcie lifted her head and looked to her right. She only had time to see the first few in a long line of people similarly bound being herded over the crest of the dune and back down toward the edge of the sea. Then a spearhead was driven into the ground right next to her eyes and a tiny foot forced her to bury her face back into the earth.

Unfortunately, no one was really saying anything, so Homer, Alcie, and Iole couldn't get a hint as to what language these creatures spoke.

They waited long minutes, their faces in the ground, before they were forced to their feet and herded to the end of the line of captives, chained four or five together. Reaching the water's edge once more, the entire group was corralled into a tight circle and forced into the sea, guarded by dozens of the small creatures, spears held tight, in a close semicircle.

Squashed together close to an outer edge, Iole could see bits of the beach and dunes in between the mass of bodies.

"I'll be right back," she whispered to Alcie.

Iole easily slipped her little hands through her manacles, then squirmed and wiggled her thin body in and around other prisoners. She stumbled once and found herself almost underwater. Only by grabbing hold of a long, dirty cloak did she regain her balance.

Making her way to the edge of the crowd of prisoners, she saw the half circle of guards and, beyond them, another, much smaller group huddled around a large metal pot. This group was not only made up of the little creatures, but there were several full-grown adult men, dressed in tattered pieces of battle gear, and one woman. As the grown men spoke to each other, the woman reached into the many sacks and pouches she carried upon herself, bringing out handfuls of various dried powders and tossing them into the cauldron. Once, one of the tiny creatures approached the group of larger men, only to receive a swift kick and a shout. Not many words, but enough that Iole understood: an odd mixture of Latin and Berber dialects.

Unexpectedly, the woman turned back to the larger men.

"Look away!" she screamed, and instantly there was a blinding flash as the contents of the pot exploded, sending a hot orange sphere rocketing into the sky, where it burst apart into a million pieces, each one arcing gracefully, flaring out, and dropping into the sea.

Less than twenty seconds later, the explosion was answered by a similar burst from the giant ship, and Iole saw a modest boat being lowered into the sea, where it moved swiftly away from the prow.

As the half circle of tiny creatures now began to round up the captives, Iole found her way back to Alcie and Homer and quickly slipped back inside her manacles.

"We're going to be taken aboard ship," she said softly as the entire group of captives moved back again onto the beach.

"Kumquats," Alcie muttered.

Suddenly, there was a great disturbance behind them and a number of the tiny creatures streamed past them into the sea. Looking over the top of the group, Homer saw that one small group of prisoners had broken away and, even though they were still chained, were heading out to deeper water. The little creatures raced out only so far, where they stood in the surf shouting furiously and shaking their spears, their shriveled bodies making it difficult to swim.

"Let them go," yelled one of the larger men, "they'll live in the bellies of sharks before the hour is out! Keep the others in line, by Jupiter's teeth, or you'll join those wretches in the sea!"

He posted a few of the creatures as sentries in case the escapees tried to come ashore, then shouted for the rest of the captive group to begin loading into the boat, which was now waiting in shallow water. One by one, the prisoners were roughly hoisted aboard, all the while being prodded and poked by the little spears. Even the youngest children and the elderly could not escape. Many of the creatures then filled the boat, taking any extra space.

When the boat was full, the rowers returned to the ship, deposited the captives, and headed back toward the beach. Twice more the boat made the crossing to ferry everyone. The third time back to the ship, Homer, Alcie, and Iole were among only a very few prisoners; the rest aboard were the full-sized men, the strange sorceress, the pot, and a large number of creatures. Almost halfway across, one creature drove his spear into Homer's leg for no reason at all. Homer, who'd not spoken since their capture, swung his other foot in an arc and kicked the creature high into the air and over the side of the boat. A huge clamor arose from the others, who were about to descend on Homer, when an enormous shark lifted out of the water, caught the airborne creature midfall, and swallowed him whole, spear and all.

The man who had spoken before on the beach, who wore more bits of armor than the others and who seemed to be in charge, let out a gargantuan laugh and held up his hand, stopping any further attack.

"Back! All of you!" he said in the strange Latin/Berber language. Then he stared at Homer for a long time.

"On my honor," he said slowly, sending a wad of yellow spittle over the side of the boat, "the Great One shall give you a kilometer squared to lift by yourself. I shall forfeit my sword if he doesn't."

Homer said nothing, not even guessing what the man could have meant. Iole started to dig her finger into Alcie's palm as the two held hands, but Alcie's squeeze let Iole know that Alcie wasn't about to utter a syllable in retort.

Coming alongside the ship, they could see hundreds of creatures at the railing and climbing the mast poles. A rope ladder was thrown over the side. Iole started up, followed by Alcie and then Homer. With their hands bound so close together, it was extremely slow going. It was only when they were almost to the railing that Homer finally had to speak.

"Whoa!"

"What?" asked Alcie, looking down at him, seeing a look of reverence come over his face.

"I've heard about her but, like, I never thought I'd actually see her," he said quietly.

"And who, for apple's sake, is *her*? Hmmm?"

"Will you two try not to be so obtrusive?" Iole whispered.

"She was built for King Hiero II." Homer was close to the railing but he was also completely rapt, so when a creature poked at him with a spear, he again whipped the creature and its spear into space without even a pause.

"They say she took a year to construct, she's got twenty banks of oars, three masts, like, eighteen hundred tons worth of cargo space, stalls for twenty horses, ginormous kitchens, and a gymnasium! So cool! I thought this ship sunk years ago—but it's her! It's the *Syracusa*!"

CHAPTER FIVE

Ismailil and Amri

The boys didn't move a muscle . . . neither of them. Pandy waited only a few seconds, hoping they would speak first and identify their language. Nothing.

"Please, get up," she said at last in Greek.

Not a twitch; only the faint breeze slightly rustling the topmost black hairs on their heads.

Pandy began to quickly run through everything she knew about the area: "Libya," the Greeks called it. It was amazing, she thought, that it stretched from the border of Egypt all the way to the great, unknown ocean to the west. And . . . ? And . . . ?

And then all she could remember was falling asleep in Master Epeus's class as he was droning on about the native Libyan people. Snooze.

With no warning at all, her mind was suddenly aware of dozens of different languages that these boys could possibly speak: Chaouia? Djerbi? Nafusi? Zenaga? All of them falling into the Berber category. What if it were another category? Without thinking she blurted out a traditional Tarifit greeting. At once the larger boy raised his face and stared at Pandy. His large, carob-colored eyes began to well up and his mouth quivered as he spoke.

"Are you death?" he asked in broken Kabyle.

As had happened so often in the last few days, Pandy spoke and understood any language she encountered because she had drunk water mixed with the ashes of a brilliant sorcerer while in the Chamber of Despair.

"No! I mean, no, I'm not death," she said to the little boy. "My name is Pandora and I come from Greece, which is . . . uh . . . that way, I think. It's far. What's your name?"

The older boy nudged the other one, who had remained stock-still.

"I am Ismailil and this is my brother, Amri," he replied. The younger boy looked up at Pandy with eyes the same beautiful brown as his brother's, only about twice the size. Pandy could plainly see he was much more terrified than Ismailil was.

She had a thousand questions, but the first thing she did was slowly put out her hand to wave very gently at Amri. These were two of the most beautiful little boys she'd ever seen. Their dark brown skin was the color of freshly tilled soil, accenting the startling whites and browns of their eyes. They each had long, wavy black hair and Ismailil at least had perfect white teeth.

"Hi, Amri." She kept her voice light and cheerful. Amri didn't even begin to smile.

All at once, the pine-nut cup fell apart with unexpected hisses and pops as several nuts underneath exploded. The boys shrieked and fled back into the shadow of the boulders as Pandy stood up, brushing and shaking nuts from her legs and clothing.

"Hey, guys?" she called after them. "Boys? Ismailil?"

She followed after them through a narrow slit in the rocks and along a twisting path deep in shadow from the rocks on either side. She soon came upon a small, open, empty space in the rock where someone had made a rather sad little camp. Two dirty mounds of rags, a small pile of drying berries (some still on their vines), a water-skin, and the tiniest pile of wood. Out of the corner of her eye, she caught the movement of something small receding from a second thin opening in the rocks.

"Ismailil? Amri?" she called softly. "I'm not going to hurt you."

Nothing.

"I have food," she said, remembering the gift of unlimited supplies of dried fruit and flatbread that Athena had given her. Reaching into her leather carrying pouch, she took out a handful of dried dates and apricots and placed them on one pile of rags. When she reached back in for more, she was surprised to find her hand on a ripe, dark red pomegranate.

"Thank you, Athena," she thought.

She settled herself midway between both openings, her back against the curved rock wall, tossing the pomegranate from one hand to the other.

"Wow!" she called out in perfect Kabyle, seemingly talking only to herself. "Does this look yummy or what? Totally dee-licious! I can't wait to bite into this. But it's way too much for me . . ."

There was a shift in the darkness from the opening.

"I wish I had someone to share this with."

She broke open the pomegranate just as two dark brown legs came into view.

"Of course," she went on, "if you don't like pomegranates, there's always apricots and dates. Maybe there's a fig lying around someplace."

To her surprise, it was the younger boy, Amri, who approached first, cautiously sidestepping his way toward the pile of rags, never taking his eyes off Pandy. He picked up an apricot and, after sniffing deeply, devoured the golden fruit in one gulp. Ismailil appeared from the opening and ran to grab his share from the pile.

"Yeah, that stuff's okay," Pandy said, trying to be as casual as possible, "but if you really want to taste something good . . . Here, catch!"

She tossed a pomegranate half to each boy. Amri leapt high to catch his while Ismailil simply held out one hand. As the brothers munched the juicy seeds, Pandy took in their appearance. They were both wearing garments similar to the togas worn by young boys back in Greece, but the fabric was heavier . . . wool, Pandy thought. Ismailil's plain white was shot through with stripes of color, and Amri's was dark red; both sleeveless, ragged, and extremely dirty. No cloaks, and Amri was missing a sandal. These boys had been here for a while.

"Can I talk to you?" Pandy asked.

Ismailil and Amri looked at each other but said nothing. Pandy got up slowly and walked toward the boys, speaking softly with every step.

"You know, I have a little brother too. His name is Xander and he's three years old. How old are you guys? Huh? That's okay, you don't have to tell me. So, like, is this where you guys are living? That's cool. You can see the stars at night and Artemis when she lets the moon loose in the sky . . ."

Pandy, now very close to the brothers, gently lowered herself onto the ground.

"It's neat, am I right?"

"I'm eight," Ismailil said, "and Amri is five."

"That's great! Those are fun ages," Pandy said.

Amri walked over to Pandy and stared at her face.

Then he pointed just underneath her left eye, to the golden teardrop—the single mark she carried from her adventure in the Chamber of Despair on her way to capture Vanity.

"This?" Pandy said, her hand reaching up. "This is . . . a . . . gift . . . from a friend. Um . . . everyone has them where I come from. Oh Gods. Uh . . . wanna touch it?"

Amri quickly stepped back and pointed at her leather carrying pouch.

"What? Oh, you want something else?"

Amri pointed at his pomegranate rind.

Pandora reached in and, to her amazement, pulled out another pomegranate, larger and redder than the first.

"Athena, you are *so* cool," she thought.

"Here you go," she said, and Amri sat on the ground next to her. "Where's your family?" she asked him.

"Amri will not answer," Ismailil said.

"How come?" Pandy asked.

"Because it was his voice that killed our mother."

For the umpteenth time in many weeks, Pandy was struck dumb. She knew that there were even more horrible, shocking, heartbreaking things yet to come, but somehow this would live with her as one of the most terrible.

"Okay," she said quietly after a moment, "why don't I tell you all about me and why I'm here. Then you can tell me whatever you want. And maybe we can help each other, okay?"

She suddenly felt much older than she actually was. There was a sense of responsibility that was settling on her shoulders. And she had no idea why.

She began slowly, telling them she was looking for something very important; her family back home was busy, so they had sent her. She told them about her friends and the magical places they'd been. She told of Delphi and Egypt. And she said that she had other friends helping her on her quest, friends who could do "special" things and that's how she'd gotten down from the mountaintop. Now she had a long journey ahead of her and maybe the boys could point her in the right direction. She had to get to someplace called Jbel Toubkal . . .

Hearing the words "Jbel Toubkal," Amri scuttled across the dirt and hid behind his brother. Pandy paused, looking at the boys.

"Okay. Um. That's about it for me. So. Why don't you like Jbel—?"

Amri's body tensed.

". . . that place?"

Amri peered up at his brother as Ismailil began.

"We live eight days' walk from here. In the highlands. Men with swords came into our village. They took my father. They chained him with everyone else. Amri and I were helping our mother gather our goats in the mountains. We heard the noise and ran back to our house. When my mother saw the men, she hid us all underneath our house. She told us to keep quiet. We watched for hours as the men took everyone. Some people tried to fight back and they were killed. Amri was hungry so my mother tried to sneak out and get some food. She told him again to be quiet, but he thought it was a game. He thought it was funny. And he wanted food. So he called out to my mother just as she was reaching for some meat and the men caught her. I hit him but it was too late. This is why he will not speak. They took her. When they left, we followed, but we went to sleep one night and when we woke up everyone was gone. We tried to find them, but Amri fell and hurt himself . . ."

It was then Pandy noticed the large gash running almost the entire length of the little boy's leg. It had not been attended to and it was becoming infected; several areas were swollen and there were pockets of pus.

"He could not walk and I could not leave him. So we stayed here."

Pandy was silent. She made the smallest motion toward her carrying pouch to retrieve the Eye of Horus, then she remembered that she'd given the magical healing amulet to Iole for her broken arm.

"How long have you been here?" she asked at length.

"Five days."

"Which way were you heading?"

Ismailil led Pandy and Amri back through the boulders to where the cup still lay in a pile of pine nuts and pointed to a pass in the western mountains. Far off in the distance, the black wall rose into the heavens, blending with it seamlessly.

"Jbel Toubkal," Ismailil said.

"The mountain is . . . is . . . that way, where that darkness is?"

Amri nodded.

"How do you know that's where they were going?"

"We would get close to the fires at night. We would listen to the men," Ismailil said. "Our parents were cold while they were warm. They spoke of someone in the mountains on the highest peak that wanted our parents. But why, we don't know."

Amri nodded.

On pure instinct, Pandy's stomach twisted itself into a knot.

She remembered where she'd heard the strange name of the mountain.

The map had already told her that she would be heading straight into the forbidding land of her uncle Atlas, for whom the mountains had been named. For fighting on the losing side in the battle between the Titans and the Olympians, Zeus had sentenced Atlas to bear the burden of the heavens upon his shoulders for eternity. Zeus had condemned him to stand forever on the tallest peak in this range, Jbel Toubkal. Cold, inhospitable, and sinister.

Suddenly, from a great distance off, they all heard the sounds of shouting and the fainter sounds of metal on metal.

The boys again retreated into the safety of the boulders, but this time they pulled Pandy with them. As the sounds became louder, the brothers raced across the clearing and into the second thin passageway until they hit a dead end. Then they began to climb up the wall in front of them, using small crevices and protrusions, toward an opening at the top, beckoning Pandy to follow. Pandy had no idea how Amri was able to climb with his leg in such horrible condition.

Reaching the top, she found the boys lying flat, inching their way toward the edge facing the road. As Pandy joined them, she could see what a tremendous vantage point they had. They could see the road approaching for at least three hundred meters and the road leading away for another two hundred.

Moving fast toward the boulders was a large group of men in light armor surrounding another, even larger group. Also with them were about a dozen extremely short, misshapen creatures of an almost reddish color waving short swords or spears. As the armed men would shift and change places, Pandy could see the other group was actually in a line, chained hand and foot, making progress somewhat slow. Someone tripped and fell as they watched. The line halted and the hapless prisoner was flogged twice and hauled back to his feet.

"Have you seen this before?" Pandy whispered. "Not just the group with your parents?"

"Since we have been here, at least three times every day," Ismailil said quietly.

Pandy looked up the road toward the west. They would have to get off the boulders quickly once the prisoners went by: the road rose steadily and anyone on the rise could easily look back and see the three of them lying on top.

Then she saw the remains of the pine-nut cup, still lying in a huge, enormous, *obvious* pile right at the entrance to the secret camp. Like a giant welcome mat.

"Gods!" she gasped. Could she get down fast enough to scatter them and get back on top before being discovered?

She was about to move when she heard a soft chattering right behind her. Twisting her body, she saw Dionysus's attack squirrel sitting on top of a boulder about three meters away, his black eyes trained on her, his whiskers twitching. Both his little hands were behind his back holding something, and before Pandy could utter a word, he flung out a tiny arm and sent a pinecone bouncing off her forehead. Then he put his claws to his mouth and gave a sharp, very short whistle, which could have been mistaken for a birdcall.

Instantly, the hillside behind the boulder cluster was blanketed with hundreds of gray and brown squirrels racing pell-mell toward the pine nuts. Pandy and the boys watched as the squirrels stuffed their cheeks with nuts until they could hold no more and then, as quickly as they appeared, they raced back up the hill and faded into the brush, leaving not one pine nut—anywhere.

Ismailil and Amri just gaped at Pandy.

"Your friends?" Ismailil asked.

"Uh—okay—sure," Pandy said, privately thanking Dionysus. It had all happened so fast and, she thought with relief, not one moment too soon. The captors and captives had just started to march past the secret opening. The brothers were scanning the people in chains.

"Do you recognize anyone?" she asked.

There was silence until Amri began to shake, tapping the rock underneath him. Ismailil followed his gaze toward the last few prisoners and a woman, older and very weak, being prodded to hurry.

"My father's mother," he gasped. "She lived in a village much farther to the east than ours."

As the captives moved off to the west and up the rise, Pandy and the boys scurried back down into the opening. Once back in the clearing, the boys watched Pandy as she contemplated the potential meaning of everything she'd just witnessed.

She remained still and silent for the rest of the afternoon, moving only once to venture outside the boulders and look at the western sky. The dark, filmy cloud seemed closer now, giving the appearance of night falling much earlier than normal. What was this? It had to be linked to everything else—the slaves, Dionysus's instructions—she was certain of it.

Finally, when true night fell, Ismailil began to rub two small sticks together for a fire. After watching him struggle for long minutes, Pandy asked Ismailil and Amri to venture out, not too far, and find just a few more branches. While they were gone, Pandy knelt down by the sad little pile of twigs and blew gently, using her special power until a thin wisp of smoke began to rise into the air and the kindling burst into flame. These boys would flee, terrified, if they knew of her secret; they'd obviously been through too much already. When the brothers returned, their arms heavy with wood, Pandy was sitting by a nice, warm fire, talking into something small she held up to her ear.

"No . . . *lots* of people, Daddy . . . like, thousands . . . yes, in chains . . . Okay, gotta go, Dad." She spotted the boys and began to whisper. "No, that's it . . . yeah, Daddy, I'm fine . . . no, they can't understand me but I still have to use my inside voice. Big-time phileo. Oh, and Daddy, will you kiss Xander for me? Yes, I'm serious. Bye."

Reaching into her carrying pouch to retrieve some flatbread, she also found a nice fresh strip of lamb, and without hesitation, a tear coursed down her cheek.

"Thank you, Athena, again," she said in her heart.

Having eaten better and feeling warmer than they had in days, the brothers immediately fell into a deep sleep, only faintly hearing Pandy say that they would be leaving early in the morning.

"She will help us find our parents, Amri, I am certain," said Ismailil, passing out.

Amri said nothing as his little eyelids closed.

Pandy rose noiselessly and tiptoed a few steps to the far side of the camp, settling herself against the side of a rock wall. She needed to attend to her evening prayers, but she didn't simply want to think them . . . she wanted to say them, whisper them if necessary, if only to feel her lips forming the words and the air moving over her teeth. She had thought of almost nothing all day but her stark new surroundings, the slavers and their chained prisoners, and of the two little strangers who had suddenly come into her life. She'd thought of her friends only twice, early that morning and when she'd described them to Ismailil and Amri. But those moments were fleeting, tinged with stress or part of an effort to coerce the brothers into trusting her. Now, alone in the glow of the fire, she ached with fear and began to beseech the gods on their behalf.

"Mighty Zeus, supreme above all . . . Wise Athena, Lovely Aphrodite, Fleet-footed Hermes . . ."

She paused.

". . . Hera, most wondrous Queen of Heaven . . ."

One by one she called out to them all, even including the lesser gods and goddesses, begging them to keep her friends alive and safe. Her words flew out of her mouth, asking the gods to please ignore Alcie's temper and sass, to keep Homer strong, and to please, please be mindful that Iole wasn't as hearty as the other two . . . that she needed special physical protection.

Then Pandy paused for a moment, using the cunning and wit she'd been developing over the past weeks to create a very special prayer, saying the words slowly and quietly, yet very clearly.

"Fierce and Merciless Ares . . . you who understand and appreciate loyalty . . . on the battlefield and at your side . . . you, whose favorite creature is the dog . . . keep watch over my precious Dido. I cannot say where he is, but I beg of you . . . *I beg of you* . . . to keep him free of harm."

(Ares, at that moment, was standing with Hades by a particular wall in Hades' apartments that wailed whenever touched, both of them pressing it in various places, listening to the sounds of souls in torment that issued forth—a favorite pastime for both gods. Over the din of agony and terror came Pandy's voice, soft and clear, in prayer. Ares paused for a second, his gaze meeting Hades' and then traveling upward toward the direction of Hera's rooms. He sighed heavily, then continued touching the wall.)

Finished, Pandy walked back to the fire and lay down, curling up close to the sleeping boys.

Pandy slept very, very little.

CHAPTER SIX

On the Syracusa

Climbing onto the deck of the massive *Syracusa,* Iole and Alcie were immediately stunned by all the noisy activity. While the captives were herded into rows and ordered to keep their eyes down, the girls managed to peek at dozens of groups of pirates behaving almost . . . merrily. Some were drinking out of large metal goblets, spilling red wine down the front of their togas. Iole saw two pirates get into a shoving match over the last drop of wine in a bottle. The skirmish, which started out good-naturedly, ended with one pirate hurling the other over the side of the ship, whereupon all the pirates in the group rushed to the railing, stared down for a moment, then threw back their heads, screaming in hysterics. Festive but discordant music was everywhere, as there were several groups of pirates playing old, broken instruments while others danced until they tripped over each other. One group was gambling, tossing odd coins, jewelry, and trinkets into a circle made of white sticks. A pirate would throw a very strange pair of dice and then, depending on the outcome, would punch another and gather up the treasures. Iole gasped when she realized that the sticks forming the gambling circle were actually human finger bones. She was loud enough that one of the pirates whispered to the others, who giggled and nodded madly. The pirate then picked up the dice and threw them low in the girls' direction. Iole watched as the dice picked up speed, bouncing over the deck until they landed at her feet. She shrieked, realizing they were dried eyeballs.

"Keep your eyes *down*!"

Iole had shifted her gaze upward in horror for only a split second, but it was enough. Swiftly, a man in nearly full battle dress was standing in front of her, carrying a sinister-looking whip.

"Look up once more and the end of my whip will be the last thing you see," said the man, his voice now close in her ear. He then turned toward the crowd.

"I am Gaius," he said, speaking to everyone, "slave master aboard this ship, and I alone will determine your fate—at least for the foreseeable future."

"Figgy apricots," Alcie muttered involuntarily.

"I have equal skill in removing tongues, maiden," said Gaius, thrusting his whip under Alcie's chin and forcing her head upward, her eyes looking directly into his, seeing nothing but hatred. He yelled over his shoulder, "Isn't that correct, Primus?"

"Muh-huh," mumbled a glum-looking pirate, standing close by.

"Primus interrupted me once," Gaius said, never taking his eyes from Alcie, small flecks of spittle in the corners of his mouth, "and I was telling a story about my mother. He won't do it again. So I'd listen if I were you. Because you won't need a tongue where you're going."

Alcie, her head raised, was able to see that at least a hundred pirates and a greater number of tiny creatures, hanging from the mast ropes, clustered on top of the guard towers, surrounded them. Then she noticed that all the men were completely bald . . . hairless, actually; not an eyebrow, not a whisker. Iole had noticed it as well, but she was also noticing something more important: these pirates were calling each other by Roman names and one of them had used the name "Jupiter," the Roman name for Zeus. She knew that the Roman Empire had spread as far south as the northern part of the African continent, so that meant that this was a whole band of Roman soldiers who had turned pirate. "But why?" she wondered.

"Where you're going," Gaius now addressed the captives, "you'll need only the sorry muscles of your arms and backs. We've been given free license to do with you what we will, as long as your backs arrive in good condition. Let's see how many of you can keep yourselves intact until we reach our destination. Now, what shall we do with each of you . . ."

Gaius moved to the head of the rows and began to walk slowly down each line.

"Galley. Oar room. Oar room. Hold. Oh, this one gave us trouble, didn't he? Chain him to the railing. Oar room. Stable."

Suddenly, he stopped in front of Homer.

"Exalted Juno," Gaius said, gazing up, "the Great One will put quite a value on your head. Look at me, youth!"

But Homer stared straight ahead.

"Too proud to look at your betters, eh?" Gaius sneered. "*Chain him to the prow*! You don't want to look at me, let us see how you like looking down into the sea for a day or two."

Three large men grabbed Homer as another approached with a heavy chain.

"Wait!"

A voice Alcie thought she recognized cut through the din on deck.

"I'll take him."

A solitary figure moved through the band of creatures. A black-haired, black-browed man who, Alcie had thought only days ago, wouldn't know a smile if one popped up out of the ocean and landed at his feet.

It was the captain of the *Peacock,* the ship on which

they'd left Greece bound for Egypt . . . the ship that had been completely destroyed.

"You'll take nothing, wretch," Gaius sputtered. "Now get back to the helm of this ship before I throw you into the arms of Neptune. And no one will fish you out this time!"

(Iole knew now she was right: Neptune was the Roman name for Poseidon.)

"Then you'll have no one to guide this vessel. Since you pirates have killed her entire crew and not one of you can control her, you'll let me have this youth or, by Zeus, in the dead of night I'll lay her on the rocks and then we'll see how you fare with . . . the Great One."

Gaius looked as if he were about to explode—literally.

"I need help with the charts. None of you can read. Most of you can barely speak. He looks like he can read. Can you read, youth?"

"Yes, sir," Homer replied.

"Then follow me. And those two maidens as well. I need cabin slaves."

Without even a backward glance, the captain strode off back across the deck the way he came. Still chained, Iole and Homer immediately began to follow; Alcie looked around, not quite sure what had just happened.

"Alcie, come on!" Iole called back, glimpsing Gaius's face, looking like he'd just been slapped.

Alcie caught up as quickly as she could and the three

followed the captain to a short set of stairs leading below deck, down a narrow corridor to two doors directly opposite each other.

"You maidens, in here," he said, showing them into a small cabin. Alcie and Iole rushed inside as the door was closed behind them and Homer's footsteps faded as he trailed behind the captain.

"*Cabin slave!*" Alcie squealed. "Black, rotting *pears*! What do I know about being a cabin slave? I've never done washing! I think I made up my pallet once when our house slave was sick. I would rather die than *touch* someone's soiled . . . unmentionables."

"Alcie—"

"And I really can't cook, Iole. I know I bragged about how good I was once when I brought some fried chicken parts to school for lunch and you and Pandy wanted some and I said I made them, but it was our kitchen slave, and she only let me watch while she—"

"Alcie!" Iole said, sitting on one of the two pallets in the room. "Calm down. My conjecture is that we won't be slaves at all. He said that to liberate us from the pirates. Hermes only knows what *they* would have us do. He said it to keep us safe."

"Safe?" Alcie cried. "Do you trust him? What's he doing being the captain of *this* ship?"

"Saving his own life, I'm certain," Iole said. "Alcie, did you look around us? There were plenty of other people, stronger and better suited to serve him, if that's what he wanted. And he knows Homer's not a chart reader. But he remembers us and, thank Athena, he's taken pity. He separated us to keep us alive."

"You think?"

"I think."

An hour later, the captain returned and removed the manacles and chains on the girls' hands and ankles, mumbling something under his breath that both Alcie and Iole heard as "senseless and cruel to use adamant on children."

"You are to stay here," he ordered as he was leaving the cabin. "I'll have Homer bring you food and fresh linens. Don't venture on deck except when I accompany you and don't go exploring anywhere the way you all did on the *Peacock*. Especially on this end of the ship. It's too dangerous and I won't be responsible." He paused on his way out.

"Iole," he said, turning his head ever so slightly, "I remember you on the *Peacock* and the fuss you made with my cook—I'll try to see you don't get anything with meat."

"Thank you—"

But he was gone.

For the next three days Alcie and Iole confined themselves to their tiny room, keeping as quiet as possible, which was difficult at times because one or the other would think about Pandy and begin sobbing wildly. Iole was almost paralyzed with one bout of crying that wracked her little body so much that Alcie, terrified, just held her close until Iole fell asleep. Iole woke to find Alcie sniffling, then crying, which built into abject weeping, so much that Iole threw her arms around Alcie until she stopped. And then they both started crying again.

They prayed daily, sometimes hourly, to Athena because she knew how hard Pandy was trying to be wise, and to Artemis because she was the protector of young things, and to Apollo to heal Pandy if she were hurt or sick. They even prayed to Hephaestus because they both remembered how he had blushed when Pandy had impulsively kissed him on the cheek after receiving the magical net. Lastly, they prayed to Hades not to let her enter the underworld. They asked him to have Cerberus, his terrible three-headed guard dog, chase Pandy away if her soul approached Hades' gates.

Their prayers went unanswered, for all they knew. There were no signs, no indication that anyone was listening.

"Maybe they only listen to Pandy," Alcie said, staring straight ahead, her afternoon prayers long finished.

"I don't think they want to be obvious," Iole said, standing up, then helping Alcie to her feet.

"Like letting us drive the Sun Chariot isn't obvi— Prunes, Iole, what's going on?"

"What?"

"You pulled me up off the floor? And, I—I can look at you!"

"You've been looking at me for almost thirteen years."

"Yeah, but now I don't have to look down so far to see you. I think you've grown a full two centimeters. And you've gotten stronger."

"Oh, that," Iole said nonchalantly. "Well, it's to be expected, certainly. I mean, you know, changes. I'm not surprised at all."

But she turned away from Alcie and, as secretly as she could, joyously pounded the air with her fist, mouthing, "Thank you, Aphrodite!"

The pirates were busy with more raids along the eastern coast of Hispania and bringing more prisoners aboard ship. No one took too much notice when Alcie and Iole went on deck each night, in the company of the captain as cabin slaves should be, for a daily dose of fresh air. Only once did a pirate approach them to offer a sip from a jug of wine.

"Yuck and no *thank* you," Alcie said.

"Jupiter's armpits," the pirate slurred, moving off. "Just trying to be friendly."

On deck, Alcie and Iole were able to look about and thought the whole scene, each night, was almost a dream. The ship was cloaked in a white fog through which could be seen filmy orange balls of light as the pirates were burning small fires on the deck.

"Isn't that just slightly dangerous?" Iole asked the captain.

"Just slightly," he replied.

The orange glow illuminated terrified prisoners chained to the railing, the number growing each night, but the fog had descended so low that the girls could really only make out the captives' legs.

They heard notes played on the old instruments, followed by someone striking up a song. If the singer was off-key, usually this was followed by a sharp yell, a short scream, and a splash. Then silence.

"They like singing, but they demand perfect pitch," the captain mused.

But it was the tiny reddish creatures that were the most astonishing. They were asleep high overhead; hundreds clinging to the ship's ropes by a hand or a knee. Others were clustered in tight bunches on top of the guard towers.

"I've never seen anything like it," the captain said, seeing Alcie and Iole staring up, "they want to be high. As high as they possibly can. It's like they've been trained. I don't know what happened to them."

Three times a day, Homer was sent to the galley for meals for the captain and the girls. It was only when Homer was delivering the food that he and Alcie were able to exchange a few words:

"Hi."

"Hi."

"Here."

"Thanks."

"Gotta go."

"Bye." Which was often followed by Alcie sticking her head out into the corridor and whispering, "Homie."

Alcie and Iole were restricted to their cabin during the day. When they weren't sleeping, crying, praying, trying to figure out how to get out of their predicament, deciding the worst way to be killed by pirates, or speaking of Pandy and all the things that might have happened to her, Alcie and Iole were having one long conversation of a very different sort.

"Who, might I query, is *Homie*?"

"Um—what's a query?"

"It's a question."

"Can't you say 'I have a question'?"

"Don't change the subject."

"Okay. Prunes. What was the question, again?"

"You're being obdurate and obfuscatory!"

"I'm not! I don't think."

"You're keeping something from me."

"Dried dates! Now I'm mad!"

Then both would simply stop speaking—until one or the other started praying or crying about Pandy.

But on the afternoon of their fourth day aboard, Iole was being more persistent than usual.

"I'm one of your best friends, in case you weren't aware! Don't even think about denying it. And best friends are supposed to confide in each other."

"You don't have to know everything. Can't I just have a little secret to myself?"

"Fine," Iole said, then she paused. "I know what it is anyway."

"What is it?"

"Never mind, I just know."

Alcie was so disconcerted by this that she chased Iole all over the room, until the two girls began to laugh wildly. It was almost exhilarating to finally be able to release some of the anger and tension of the past few days, that Iole didn't even mind when Alcie ultimately tripped her, sending Iole sprawling onto one of the pallets, where Alcie sat on her back until she turned pink.

"Your hair is getting really long," Alcie said.

"So is yours. And you're getting heavy. Really heavy." Iole's words were muffled because she was facedown in the pallet linens.

Alcie began to absentmindedly braid Iole's dark brown hair while she sat on her, when suddenly the ship gave a tremendous lurch, followed by a long shudder and (they thought) a groan. Then silence. Then the old wood, all the beams, sidewalls, and floorboards at once, began to creak incessantly. Then silence.

Alcie leapt off of Iole's back. They both remained stock-still for a minute. Then they heard heavy footsteps in the corridor, which stopped just outside the door to Homer's cabin, directly across from theirs. Homer had been out all day, Alcie was sure of it, and was just now returning to his cabin. Waiting a full ten seconds, Alcie opened the door and collided with Homer, standing in the doorframe. She felt the most astounding and unusual electric shock run through her body.

"Uh—"

"Uh—"

"Okay," Iole said from behind, "our cabin. Hurry before anyone sees!"

Alcie and Iole picked the cushions off the floor and sat on one of the two small pallets in the cabin while Homer sat on the other, after turning it right-side up.

"Do you know what just happened?" Alcie asked.

"Yes, do you know why the boat just lurched so violently?" Iole followed.

"Why is everything overturned?" Homer asked, unaware of their questions. "What were you guys doing?"

"Oh, that. Uh . . . exercising," said Alcie.

Iole just rubbed her sides.

"Well," Homer whispered, "you know I've, like, basically been in only two places since we were kidnapped: my cabin and the captain's quarters."

As Homer was talking, Alcie noticed that he wasn't really looking at them . . . his gaze was focused just past her and his voice, even in a whisper, seemed to catch in his throat.

"Now, I know Jealousy and Vanity are already in the box, that is if Pandy is still alive, and the box didn't get smashed or something."

"May I just say that you have the most delicate, sophisticated, and urbane way of putting things," Iole said.

"But you also said something," Homer went on, completely oblivious, "about having to find some lesser evils. And you didn't know where to look for them?"

"Correct," Iole said.

"Well, I was just looking at some scrolls in the captain's cabin, and there's—uh—something you might want to see."

CHAPTER SEVEN
On Mount Olympus

"Ow!"

There was a crash of glass, followed by a bark, then a yelp . . . then soft whimpering. A pungent perfume filled the hallway.

Demeter, who normally hurried anyway when summoned to Hera's apartments, now broke into a run, shaking spring grasses and flowers loose from her hair.

"I will *teach* you!" Hera's voice ricocheted off the marble walls. "I will show you just what happens to mangy, flea-bitten—"

"Hera! What . . . ?!" Demeter cried, arriving at the large entryway just in time to see Hera send the shards of glass from the shattered perfume bottle flying upward, cementing them into the ceiling.

The Queen of Heaven was standing in the middle of her salon, a small tear in her blue robes about halfway up her rather sizable leg. She raised her left arm, her index finger twirling the air. In a corner of the room, Dido was pinned on his belly to the wall, spinning around in time with Hera's finger. As Demeter watched, Hera forced Dido up the wall and across the ceiling, toward the shards of glass.

"Stop!"

Hera was stunned. Demeter never raised her voice unless it was time for her daughter, Persephone, to descend back down to the underworld to join her husband, Hades. Then Demeter made her opinion known, Hera recalled. But now . . .

"Hera, put the dog down!" Demeter cried.

"He bit my leg!" Hera said, but she stopped moving Dido across the ceiling.

"Hera, *please* put the dog down. You know what will happen if any harm comes to him."

Hera stuck out her lower lip and pouted for about ten seconds.

"Oh . . . fine!"

With a squeal, Dido dropped to the floor. In a flash, Demeter caused a large patch of soft grass to grow a full meter high right underneath, so Dido fell onto a cushy green pillow. He lay there stunned for a moment.

Hera made a move toward him.

"Hera . . . darling . . . back away from the dog," Demeter said softly but firmly.

"Oh, pooh!"

Demeter went to check on Dido as Hera, with a flick of her wrist, tore the glass shards out of the ceiling and reconstructed the perfume bottle on her dressing table.

As Demeter approached, Dido gave a growl; then, seeing it was not his tormentor, licked her hand in gratitude. Quickly he leapt up and slunk into a far corner.

"I'm sure he was only playing." Demeter turned to see Hera, now standing out in the hallway, arms spread wide, blowing mightily back into the room. Above Demeter's head, the escaped perfume was collecting into an amber mist, which condensed into a dense cloud and floated over the perfume bottle. After a moment, the cloud began to rain, drop by drop, into the bottle until all the perfume was replenished.

"No, he was not playing," Hera said, approaching Demeter. "He plays with you, remember? He doesn't play with me."

"Well, you stole him from his mistress. You can't be surprised that he's not overly fond of you."

"I think I can, yes." Hera sulked. "I take excellent care of him."

"You feed him scraps, you don't let him exercise, and he's lonely. How is that taking excellent care?"

"I haven't *killed* him, okay?"

"Pardon me, your generosity is boundless."

"I just wanted to sprinkle a little perfume on him. He's begun smelling up my fragrant rooms and I'll be a mortal slave before I give him a bath. So I just tried to do something nice . . . and he bit me."

"Yes." Demeter sighed. "You said. Well, it's over now."

"He's still stinky."

"When all are asleep, I shall give him a bath in my rooms. All right? Will that make you feel better?"

"Hmmm . . . I think it will."

"Now, dearest Hera, why did you summon me?"

"What news?"

"Everyone's keeping rather quiet, you know."

"Are you telling me you've found out *nothing* in the last few days?" Hera spat.

"Well, as I told you, when Pandy fell from the chariot, Dionysus actually sobered up and sequestered himself away for a bit, no bacchanals, no revelry, and he canceled his wine delivery. The only thing I can tell you is that I saw him talking to a large squirrel the other day."

"Squirrel . . . hmm, I see."

"And," Demeter continued, "I know Hephaestus has been talking with the spirit of Cassandra—"

"Cassandra?"

"She was the maiden that Apollo gave the gift of prophecy to, but when she refused his love, he cursed her so that no one would believe her predictions. Sort of messed up the Trojan War . . ."

Hera glared at Demeter.

"*I know who she is!* I'm just wondering why he would be talking to her spirit."

"Apparently, she contacted him. Something's happening with the other three on the *Syracusa* and she told him to be prepared. He just can't decide whether to believe her or not. Look, darling . . . light of all our lives . . . there's nothing you can do about it anyway. Not without all of them knowing that you *know* something and then they'll rat you out to your husband and he'll make a rare visit to your rooms, see the dog, and fly into a teeny-tiny rage. Let it go for now. You *know* what Pandora has coming up. Five days of it. If that doesn't kill her, well, then nothing will. Now, I must get a moment's rest before I give Dido his bath. I shall see you presently."

With a kiss blown to Hera, she was gone.

"Let it go . . . ," mused Hera. "Hmmm . . . I suppose she's right. Huh?"

Hera whipped around, suddenly possessed with the sensation that she was not alone.

No one was there. Nothing was amiss. Everything was in its place: the reclining couch, the dressing table, the silver candelabra, the hairbrushes, the knickknacks, Dido on the floor in the corner.

All was as it should be.

She did not notice as the eyes on the small bust of

her husband, Zeus, on the table next to her magnificent sleeping pallet, stopped following her movements and returned to their original black marble.

She pondered for a moment and then shook her magnificent red hair.

"Oh . . . silly."

Feeling a little better, slightly more certain of her position and, therefore, a touch more benevolent, she turned her attention again to the rebuilt perfume bottle and then to the cowering dog.

"Let's try it again, shall we? Here, doggy!"

CHAPTER EIGHT
Minor Operation

Two days of walking had taken Pandy and the boys just slightly less than twenty kilometers westward. "Not far at all," Pandy thought.

Aware that the filmy black wall was slowly nearing with each step, they skirted to the side of the main road through the pass to Jbel Toubkal and the home of her uncle Atlas, hiding from kidnappers with a heavy complement of prisoners heading back into the mountains one moment; the next, fleeing from a raiding party on its way out to pillage. They traveled at night, dusk, or dawn, never nearing the campfires or only getting close enough to eavesdrop on the kidnappers' conversation.

The first night on the road, Pandy decided to tell the boys all about the shells.

"Okay," she said, running her finger down the lip of her shell, "now listen."

On the other end, she heard her father's voice clearly, and Pandy held the conch up to Ismailil.

"Say 'Hello, Prometheus,'" she whispered.

When Prometheus answered, Ismailil's eyes grew huge.

"Magic! Magic!" he said, smiling broadly.

"Yeah, kinda, but good magic," she said, taking the shell back.

Pandy told her father about the black wall, the prisoners, and Jbel Toubkal.

"I think we can hide from the kidnappers, but I have no idea what I am gonna do when I get to, like, wherever it is. But Daddy, I'm certain it's where Uncle Atlas lives. I've never met him, so he probably won't recognize me—"

The line began to crackle, then went dead.

"Daddy . . . ?"

Pandy shook the shell.

"Daddy?"

She tried using the shell again. Nothing.

"It's probably the mountains," she said to the boys. "I'll try again tomorrow."

They spent a great deal of time in hiding, which was the only time Pandy could check Amri's wound. His leg was now so bad that Pandy didn't know how the little boy stood, let alone trudged the steep inclines. Ismailil tried to carry his brother, but that got all of them nowhere fast. Pandy did a little better but needed to rest often with his extra weight on her back. For his part, Amri made not a sound, trying to be very brave; it was only when Pandy saw a single tear slide down his cheek did she realize the pain he must be in. The wound was deeper than she first thought, and now the leg was turning a slight green. Maybe it's just days and days of dirt, Pandy tried to reassure herself, hoping that underneath, Amri's leg wasn't *that* bad, but she'd seen the color before: playing behind the Athens Free Clinic one day, she'd seen a hulky assistant healer carry out a single greenish leg that had been freshly severed from its owner and toss it onto the garbage pile. Pandy knew she simply didn't have it in her to remove a little boy's leg. That was asking too much.

Clambering up the side of the hill in the late afternoon, hidden behind a large cedar tree, the boys watched another group of passing prisoners for anyone they recognized while Pandy thought only of the Eye of Horus, desperately wishing she had it with her. That led to thoughts of Alcie, Iole, and Homer: what had happened to them? Were they alive? Where was Dido? Was Hera even *feeding* him? And then the realization that always ended these thoughts: none of this would have happened if not for her.

Everything was her fault.

Suddenly, Amri cried out. Not very loud, but loud enough that Ismailil put his hand over his brother's mouth and everyone froze—almost. Several large red fire ants had crawled up Amri's leg and into his wound. The little boy tried to squirm but Ismailil held him fast.

The line of prisoners was almost out of sight, but a single slaver, bringing up the rear of the line, stopped short and turned around, his head cocked to one side.

At this, Amri became still, his breath coming through Ismailil's fingers in short bursts, tears streaming down his small face.

The slaver stood for a long time just staring at the hillside, scanning the bushes and rocks for any movement, listening for any sound—focusing particularly on the large cedar trees high to the right. Only a shout from far up at the head of the line caused him to turn around and move ahead, running to catch up with the others.

When the group had rounded a curve in the road, Pandy crawled over to Amri, now frantically beating at his wound, and poured some water from her skin over his leg, washing the ants away. Reaching down for her cloak to dry him off, her hand brushed against her carrying pouch and she felt something oddly shaped and hard.

The bust of Athena. The miniature replica of the

goddess, a gift from the Wise One herself. When Pandy was in trouble, or completely dumbfounded like she was now, she could seek help by questioning the bust and Athena would answer through it.

"Now, don't be afraid, okay," she said to the boys as she brought out the bust. "I think this will help."

Remembering Athena's warning that she could only ask a question once and that the statue's tiny tongue would stick a little, she thought carefully before she spoke, switching to her native Greek.

"Great Athena—"

The bust's lids flew open, revealing again Athena's beautiful green eyes.

"How can I heal this little boy's leg?"

Immediately, the mouth began to move, the little tongue clicking and clacking as if it were glued with honey. But Pandy caught every word, every herb—"fenu-*click*-greek, stinging nettle." To her surprise, she knew all of them. Then came the instructions—"gather"—*click*—"mix a dry poult-*click*-ice." Although, the last one made no sense: "Sew."

Sew *what*?

The wound—had to be.

With what?

When the bust stopped speaking, she stowed it away, told the boys to stay put, and began checking the hillside. The nettles and the knit-bone she found right off.

But she couldn't locate the fenugreek, charcoal, or the Ulmus rubra.

"Come on, come on," Pandy began mumbling. The bust wouldn't have said it if she wouldn't be able to find it. The gods *couldn't* be that cruel. Not with a little boy's leg at stake.

Suddenly, a bush ten meters up the hillside began to glow with a bright red halo. Pandy hiked up and picked some of the light green fenugreek leaves. Then a pile of black stones much farther up began to glow, and Pandy, with a great deal of difficulty, panted her way up the hillside and gathered up a handful of black charcoal. She needed one last ingredient: *Ulmus rubra*. She looked for something glowing. Nothing. But she was learning the ways of the gods: they *were* helping, most definitely, but more often than not she would have to work for every bit of aid they gave, especially from Athena, who, Pandy sensed, expected just a little bit more out of her than everyone else.

Fine.

Pandy searched higher and farther. Finally, she spotted a small red glow way above her on the very top of the mountain, surrounding a small tree that hadn't been there a second ago, she was sure of it.

"Okay, just watch me!" she huffed.

Picking and clawing her way past thinning brush, she found herself on a steep incline of loose stones, overhanging rock ledges, and—she bit her tongue, not saying a word and not even *thinking* anything—snow. Icy patches covered the ground precisely where she needed to climb. She dug her hands and feet into the snow, moving like an animal ever higher. Twice she slipped and slid back, once coming so close to the edge of a sheer drop, she actually *did* bite her tongue. She scraped her knees and bruised her shins. She stubbed three toes, hit her head on an overhang, scratched her hands, and broke two nails down to the quick. At last, out of breath, she reached the top of the mountain and the tree, a beautiful spring green underneath the red glow. Plucking several of the largest leaves, she turned and realized that she would have had a view of almost the entire Atlas Mountain range.

Except that now most of it was cloaked by the filmy black wall.

And Jbel Toubkal was nowhere to be seen.

She did notice that the wall, again, didn't seem to actually touch the earth, and the ground underneath (what she could see in the fading light) was pale, growing whiter as it stretched away.

"More snow," she sighed, looking at the kilometers of ground before her, knowing their destination was at least a week's walk away, if not more. But, more importantly, she saw the campfires burning dully far below and realized that the slavers were closer than she thought—and their numbers were massive. She turned to face the deadly descent back down and found the rock now cut through by a smooth path that wound its way in a serpentine back and forth across the mountain.

"Thank you, thank you," she whispered as she hurried back to the boys. Then, as she was almost upon them, it hit her. She knew what she could use to sew the wound.

"I've said it before and I'll say it again. Thank you," she practically sang.

She brought out the blue marble map Hera had given her at the beginning of her quest. Using it as an ordinary bowl (knowing that it wouldn't begin spinning without her tears), Pandy mixed all the herbs into a dry poultice, following Athena's instructions exactly. She prayed earnestly and fervently to Apollo in Greek. Then she cleaned Amri's wound of the dried blood and pus, telling him in Kabyle what a really good patient he was being and asking his brother to tell him a joke. Ismailil just looked at Pandy as if she were insane.

"No jokes?" she asked, forcing a smile. "Okay, here's one my dad used to tell all the time before my mother made him stop: Plato and Socrates walk into a tavern . . ."

As she carefully added drops of water to make a paste of the herbs, she had a flash of herself, no more than two months ago, dragging home from school, being lazy, napping, dawdling, flopping around, thinking she was bored out of her skull. Could she ever have imagined herself working now with such speed and focus, trying to save a little boy's leg in another part of the world? Not in a gazillion years.

Then Pandy used her power over fire and blew up and down the length of the wound, completely sterilizing it.

"Rope," she said, "come to me."

The flap of her carrying pouch flipped back and the coil of enchanted rope, yet another gift from Athena, flew into her hands. Ismailil and Amri were too astonished to even be afraid.

Confused for a split second, she began to speak the next part in Kabyle, but realized just in time that she couldn't, not without frightening the boys even further.

"Small enough to *sew skin*," she said in Greek.

Instantly the rope shrunk itself so small that it all but disappeared.

"Sew Amri's leg!"

With the speed of a surgeon, the rope, now no thicker than a hair, wound its way in and out of the little boy's leg, completely sealing the wound. Amri would tell his children years later that it was like being tickled by a crab.

Pandy applied the poultice she'd made to the beautifully sewn wound. Then she took her spare toga and ripped off the hem, knowing that this was a much better use for it anyway, and wrapped Amri's leg.

"And that is that!" she said.

Thirty seconds later, after remaining silent for the entire procedure, both Ismailil and Amri burst into tears.

"Hey, what the—?" Pandy cried. "No, it's okay now."

But the brothers, although they were quiet, simply wouldn't stop.

"Sheesh. Boys."

CHAPTER NINE

A Book of Letters

Homer led them all down the long passage leading to the captain's quarters. Immediately, Alcie and Iole knew something was not right. Instead of leading straight off into the ship, the passageway now twisted ever so subtly. The wooden walls had become darker, and small fractures ran through all of the beams. As they neared the captain's cabin, the fractures in the wood became large enough to expose lamplight from the cabins on the other side of the corridor. Splinters the size of swords stuck out from some of the joists, and the wall sconces were tilted. Every so often, there was a great shudder, as if the *Syracusa* herself were sighing.

"What's going on?" Alcie asked.

"I don't know, but whatever it is, it started in the captain's cabin."

"Homer, do you think the captain can be trusted?" Alcie asked.

"Absolutely," Homer answered, but his voice was far away. "He hates this. He told me he wished that he had actually been sent straight to the underworld when the *Peacock* was destroyed. But instead he just floated on a plank of wood for days until the *Syracusa* picked him up. He's thought more than once about ramming the ship— destroying her somehow—but he doesn't want to risk the lives of all the prisoners. And it's, like, an amazing ship."

"Are you really helping the captain with the charts and maps?" asked Alcie, trying to get him to just look at her.

"I guess so," Homer replied. "There were a couple of charts he told me to stay away from, so I've just been looking at currents and coastlines and stuff."

Just then, the ship groaned and rolled hard to one side, and they all went crashing heavily into the passageway wall. Homer, who had instinctively thrown up his hand to steady himself, let out a loud cry.

"What's wrong, Homie—er?" said Alcie.

"Nothing—it's just my hand. Where it bit me," he said.

"Where *what* bit you?" Iole asked.

"This thing, you know? The thing I wanted you to see."

"Let me see your hand!" Alcie said sharply. She quickly added in a softer tone, "Please."

He held out his right hand: a chunk of flesh was missing from the meaty side of his thumb, almost down to his wrist. The edges of the wound were jagged, as if he'd been bitten by something with dozens of tiny serrated teeth. He'd tried to staunch the wound by wrapping it tightly in the folds of his robe, but using his hand to keep himself righted after the ship had rolled had started the flow of blood again.

"Gods—," Iole said, genuinely alarmed, "we've got to stop the bleeding. The Eye of Horus . . . it's in my pouch back in the cabin."

"It's okay. It'll stop in a moment—it's just muscle," he protested. "I got sliced worse than this back in gladiator school. I really need to show you something."

Abruptly, Iole turned her head in the direction of the captain's quarters.

"Listen—"

Every so often, there was a light whirring or whistling sound followed by the short, sharp squelch of splintering wood. Occasionally, the whirring was followed by a soft thud. After several thuds, the end of Iole's nose tingled ever so slightly.

"Do you smell that?"

"Something spoiled . . . like bad fruit or juice," Alcie said.

"It's more like . . . like . . . burned hair!" said Iole, recalling their first adventure capturing Jealousy. "That's how I smelled after almost being roasted on the Altar of the Oracle of Delphi!"

Homer was now rubbing his hand vigorously within the folds of his robe.

Then he burst into tears.

"Whoa," said Alcie under her breath.

"Uh, Homer, what's going on?" Iole asked.

"I don't know," he moaned, his eyes shut very tight, grasping his wounded hand and rocking his whole body so that it bumped into the wall. "I just feel really— really—um—sad."

"Homer . . . look at me," Iole said. "Tell me everything that happened before you came to our cabin. Okay? This is—oh, what's your word—*totally* important."

He opened his eyes, tears running down his cheeks.

"Well, when I came into his quarters this morning, the captain was gone. But he wanted me to look at the map of the Balearic Islands, so I went to get it, and, um, one of the charts that the captain didn't want me to see was hanging down a little ways off of its rod. I just tried to ignore it, you know? Then the ship rolled way to one side . . . but gently, like normal . . . nothing like what's happening now . . . and the chart fell down a little farther. I didn't want the captain to think that I had looked at it, so I tugged on it a little and tried to send it rolling back up. But when I did, it unfurled all the way and this thing fell out."

"Thing?" said Alcie.

The *Syracusa* shuddered so violently at that moment

that they thought they heard something snap on the deck overhead.

"It was a book . . . just a little book," Homer said, his lower lip quivering so badly, his words were almost lost. "So I, like, went to pick it up—to put it back, you know? Then it jumped at my hand and bit me. And then some . . . things flew out of the book. That's when I came to get you."

Alcie and Iole stared at Homer for a moment, his face now turned toward the wall in abject despair. Alcie reached forward and touched Homer lightly on his unhurt hand.

"Come on."

The three of them moved toward the captain's quarters. Not wanting to be hindered at any time by a bolted door, the pirates had purposefully removed it.

"I think—maybe you're gonna want to bend down," said Homer, lowering himself to the floor as they rounded a corner.

"Why?" asked Iole.

"Because there's things flying all over the room and sticking in the walls."

Sure enough, several arrows were sticking out in the passageway wall directly across from the door. It was as if someone were shooting them out from inside the room.

Alcie and Iole ducked down and crawled the rest of

the way to the door. Alcie stuck her head around the doorframe.

The walls of the small room were covered with arrows: sticking into wooden chairs and open charts and protruding up from the floor. There were arrows on the captain's sleeping cot and stuck into the large wooden chest where he kept his private articles. But there were also several small sheets of parchment lying on the floor, a dark-edged hole burned into the center and a thin wisp of smoke rising off of each one.

Suddenly an arrow whizzed by Alcie's ear and zinged into the wall behind her. It gave off a sound like a low moan.

After it had stopped jiggling up and down, she quickly yanked it from the wall and found it was not an arrow, in the usual sense, at all.

It was a tightly rolled piece of parchment. Alcie held it to her nose, coughing a little at the smell of burned hair. She began to unroll the paper, over Iole's protestations.

She had unrolled about six or seven centimeters, revealing a beautifully scripted letter, when a clump of something stringy dropped out, exploded with a white-hot *pop* in midair, and landed on the floor. The pungent smell of burned hair again filled the narrow passageway, causing everyone to gasp.

Two more letter-arrows shot through the doorway

and landed in the back wall; these two flew with high-pitched feminine wails of different notes—almost as if they were wailing in harmony.

Fully unrolling the letter still in Alcie's hand, they saw it was either faded or discolored as if blackened by a fire. They could make out only a few random words; words like "desperate," "unbelievable," "nightmares," and "lonely."

"Moldy green melons!" said Alcie, reading as much as she could. "This person was not having a good time."

At the very bottom were the words "My breaking heart still clings— —beloved, Latona."

Another letter-arrow shot out of the room with a deep low-throated yowl, but this one banged off a bronze shield hanging in the passageway. It fell to the floor with a soft thud and quickly unrolled itself flat. This time, when the stringy substance hit the air, it ignited and started a small fast-burning fire in the center of the letter. The scent of burning hair again filled the passageway as the letter went up in flames.

Iole reached up and pulled another letter out of the wall, nearly grazed by one incoming.

"She must have included a lock of her hair in every letter," Iole said, unrolling the letter fully. "But why? And who is she?"

The letter was in much the same condition as the first. But as Iole had unrolled it, certain words seemed to fade or obscure and other words and phrases became more legible. "Predicament," "gone so long," and "disease of the heart," popped out in full black ink.

They heard a sudden chatter inside the captain's room and Alcie stuck her head around the doorframe once again.

On the floor, underneath the table in the center of the room, lay a small leather-bound book. It was opening and closing slowly, revealing hundreds of small ivory-colored teeth set in two rows around the top and bottom edges. But it wasn't opening and closing all by itself. They saw two tiny figures inside the book: a woman with long, long hair and a small boy. Both were made of a transparent silvery-blue substance and moved like steamy fluid, leaving trails of silver-blue in the air behind them. They were talking to each other in squeaky, high-pitched voices.

"Kumquats . . . ," said Alcie softly.

Both the woman and the boy were pushing on the inside cover of the book, trying to get it to stay open. Finally, they flipped the heavy leather cover backward and the small boy, no bigger than Alcie's fist, jumped on top. It was then that Alcie saw the teensiest set of wings on the boy's back.

The boy squeaked something to the woman, who picked up a small bow from inside the book and handed it to him. Walking to the top of the book, she ripped a single page from the inside. She rolled the page into a small cylinder and gave it to the boy. He quickly placed it on his bow and shot the "arrow" through the door and into the passageway wall. The two then fell back laughing, tumbling down into the now hollowed-out inside of the book, which allowed the leather cover to snap shut again. Then the whole process started all over.

"That's Eros!" Iole said as the arrow went moaning over their heads, crashing into the bronze shield.

"The God of Love?" Alcie whispered, pinching her nose as the hair inside the arrow ignited.

"I'm sure of it," Iole said, "but Pandy told us that the gods were going to be helping her whenever they could. If she—or we—were meant to find whatever this is, then shooting letters that could kill us is not helping!"

"Iole, Eros is immortal but he's only about two years old. He's just a little baby god," Alcie countered. "He wouldn't know what he's doing."

The two shimmery figures were now pushing the book of letters farther to one side of the room in order to be able to shoot the "arrows" directly at Alcie, Iole, and Homer. However, they accidentally sent it careening into one of the support poles in the center of the cabin. Immediately, the book took a bite out of the old wood, and the ship shuddered violently again as she rolled to one side, all the beams creaking and moaning, sending a silver tray and an urn crashing to the floor.

That's when Alcie noticed other bite marks in the cabin: the walls, a table, the floor itself.

"It's eating the ship," Alcie muttered.

"What?" asked Iole.

"Or it's infecting it somehow," Alcie said, staring back at Iole. "The ship is . . . feeling it. That's why it's lurching and groaning!"

"Feeling what?"

"We have to do something!" Alcie's face was suddenly grim. "The three of us—"

"Homer's gone," Iole said. "He crawled away a while ago."

Fine, Alcie thought; she knew that having him there in his condition would probably only make matters worse.

"The two of us, then. Okay, here we go," she said, hoping that her words were sounding the way Pandy would have said them. "I'll go in and surprise them. And then . . . and then . . ."

Without warning, Alcie quickly reached up and snatched the bronze shield off the passageway wall. Another of Eros's arrows came perilously close to piercing her rear end. Then she turned and ran, yelling, into the room.

"Ahhhh!"

The two figures were so startled that Eros dropped his bow.

"Ahhhh!" they screamed together.

Then Iole rushed in.

"Ahhhh!"

"Ahhhh!"

"Get them!" Alcie yelled.

Instantly Eros took off flying around the room. With no more arrows to shoot, he began dive-bombing the girls, howling with laughter.

Alcie dropped to the floor and went after the little woman, but she was so swift that Alcie caught only handfuls of blue vapor.

"Don't touch it with your bare hands!" shouted Iole.

"Give me something!"

Iole ran to the far side of the cabin and snatched a thin fabric covering off of a pile of crates.

"Here!"

Alcie caught the cloth in the air and moved to scoop up the woman, but she was too fast and ran right under Iole's legs; Alcie tried to follow, sending both girls sprawling. Alcie chased the woman behind the pile of crates only to see her dash out the other side.

"There she goes!" yelled Iole.

"I see her!"

The figure took one moment to look behind her as she ran. She was almost clear across the room when she turned to face forward again and almost ran headfirst into the fallen silver tray, now lying against the cabin wall.

Stopping dead in her tracks, she saw her own

reflection. She put her hands up to her face, took a deep breath, and let out a moan that filled the entire cabin. It was a sound of complete, utter despair. Alcie and Iole covered their ears; Eros whizzed out of the cabin. Then the tiny woman quietly passed out, falling with a blue trail to the floor as Alcie threw the cloth, covering the figure completely.

"Now what?" asked Alcie, breathing heavily and looking desperately at Iole. "Gods!"

"Pandy has the net and the box, Alcie. We've got nothing that will hold her—it."

"Look!" Alcie crossed to the crates and picked up a small wooden box. She opened it and a tiny golden spoon fell onto the table.

"Here!"

She strode back across the room, slowly lifted the cloth, and reached for the figure.

"Not with your bare hands!" Iole said.

"Okay, like . . . duh!" Alcie said, startled, but she wrapped her hand in the cloth and very gingerly picked up the tiny woman with her thumb and forefinger and placed her in the box.

"Ta-da!"

"It doesn't have an adamant clasp, Alcie," Iole cautioned. "This thing is a lesser evil, but it still needs to go in *the* box."

"Iole," Alcie said, "we can't let her go. Whatever this

is, it's not supposed to be here. You know it and I know it. We came to help Pandy, even if she's not around, so use that stuff between your ears and—"

Alcie suddenly took in a sharp breath and went silent, almost as if she'd been turned to stone.

"Alcie?"

"Shackles."

She stared at Iole, then spoke with uncommon deliberateness, as if each word were presenting itself in her brain only one at a time.

"The captain—when he took off our shackles—he said something about how cruel it was to use them because they were . . . ."

"Adamant," Iole and Alcie said at precisely the same time.

"But it's not a net!" Iole said.

"We'll figure it out!" Alcie said, moving past her back down the corridor.

Clutching the box tightly, she raced back toward their cabin, flung open the door, and was hopping around between the sleeping pallets when Iole panted into the room.

"Gods, you run so fast now that your feet are back to normal!"

"Okay. Okay," Alcie rushed on, "we know that the net is adamant and we think that's the only thing that will capture an evil until it gets into the box. Right?"

"Righ—"

"Now, we don't have the net and we don't have *the* box. We just have an evil in a box. But we know that there are adamant shackles on this ship. So what if we got those and somehow . . . surrounded this box. She's just a tiny woman, how strong could she be, right?"

"Righ—"

"Shackles would be kept where—in the armory, right? When my dad was fighting in a war close to home and it was Take Your Daughter to Work Day, I always used to see shackles and chains in the armory. So, where's the armory on the ship?"

"I don't think it's on this end; we'd hear clanking," Iole said.

"Good thinking."

"If I were designing a ship, I'd put it in the middle: easy to get to, even weight distribution."

"Okay, let's go get—"

"Alcie," Iole cut her off, "we can't just walk into the armory. We'll be killed or chained up or Hades knows what!"

"Right. We can't both go." Alcie paused. "But if one of us were to create a diversion, then the other could sneak in behind and get the shackles. Now, I can carry heavier stuff and you're not so much of a threat—to anyone. And they probably wouldn't do much of anything to you if you act all innocent and girly. So . . ."

"So, you want to use me as *bait*?" Iole squealed. "Why am I always bait?"

"When have you ever been bait?"

"Hello! Cleopatra?"

"Okay, but don't think of it as bait!"

"That's what it is!"

"I know, but don't think of it like that. Find another big word for it, a pretty word."

Out of nowhere, they both heard shouts of "Evening meal" and heavy footsteps racing about on the main deck above their heads. Instinctively, they opened the cabin door and paused only a moment to listen to the sound of something like furious scratching coming from Homer's cabin. Clinging to the inside of the passageway, they stole up on deck.

Almost everyone, except the prisoners, was either heading for or already gathered at the back of the ship as the cook ladled out bowls of odd-smelling soup. A few pirates were already seated in small groups, eating and drinking.

"This is perfect," Alcie whispered, hearing an off-key tune and then a splash.

The two girls, darting from one guard tower to another, snuck to an opening mid-deck and down into the bowels of the *Syracusa*. Seeing no one, they peeked into several large, empty rooms: an abandoned spa now littered with makeshift pallets and trash, a library with most of the books thrown onto the floor to make room for the kidnappers' personal items. Peeking into another room, Iole caught a glimpse of the sorceress before she forced Alcie to flatten herself against the wall, putting fingers to both their lips. The sorceress, humming softly, had her back turned, her nose in a jar of something foul-smelling, and didn't notice the two girls slinking by her quarters. Scurrying along the empty passageways, they finally found the armory, full of immense weapons—those of the kidnappers and those looted from their hapless captives. Iole and Alcie went straight to the wall where hundreds of sets of shackles and chains hung on hooks, a key in each lock. Trying to be quick yet thorough in their examination, Alcie had her hands on two sturdy sets.

"Those are strong enough, I suppose," came a stern voice from behind them.

Both girls froze.

Suddenly, there was an ear-splitting clang of metal hitting metal.

Alcie and Iole glanced sideways at each other, then turned around, waiting to be slashed to ribbons.

In the center of the armory, there now stood an enormous anvil and behind it, a giant of a man. His massive arms were covered in soot, his dark brown hair flew out from his head at wild angles, and a heavy ink-black beard covered his face. He had a large gold earring in one ear, a tiny Roman helmet on his head, and a black tattoo of a woman on one arm. With an enormous arc he brought a huge hammer down upon a piece of metal with another clang that almost sent the girls to their knees.

"This pair, however, might be more to your liking," he growled, raising his hammer high once more.

"Please don't kill us," Alcie whispered.

But Iole had already begun to understand. Brown hair? Black beard? And, of course, she'd seen him before.

"Heph-Hephaestus?" she stammered.

The hammer stopped in midswing.

He dropped his head, his shoulders sagged. Slowly, he laid the hammer down on the anvil and looked sheepishly at the girls.

"What gave me away?"

"Brown hair, black beard—oh, wondrous smithy," Iole said. "And, perhaps, the giant anvil. Besides, all the other pirates are completely bald."

"Oh, bald. Right," he sighed, then gave a little hop and disappeared. Then next instant he appeared from behind the anvil, startling the girls for a second with his severely misshapen lower body no bigger than that of a tiny baby. And now, of course, he was no taller than the girls. Iole realized he'd been standing on a chair.

"Aphrodite swore that you wouldn't recognize me in this," he said, pulling the fake black beard away from his face.

"I didn't," said Alcie honestly, making him feel a little better.

"Why are you incognito?" asked Iole.

Both Alcie and Hephaestus just stared at her.

"In disguise," she clarified.

"It's a pirate ship," he said brightly, "and how much fun is *that,* I ask you? I almost never get to leave the forge, so I thought here's a chance to see how the other half lives. And anything I can do to cover this ugly face . . ."

"Oh, I wouldn't say—," Alcie spoke up.

"Enough, please don't flatter. Or lie. Doesn't suit either of you. Now, listen, we have no time. Take these."

He pulled a pair of shackles down from on top of the anvil.

"They're adamant, naturally. And I've crafted them so they'll fit around that box."

"How did you know?" Alcie asked.

"I've been watching you in the fire on my forge. I check in every once in a while. And I heard your prayers. Everyone on Olympus has, actually, but of all the gods, Zeus pays the least attention to me, and I knew I could sneak away and help this time. Here, let me have it."

Wordlessly, Alcie handed the box to Hephaestus. He held it up to his large ear. From inside could be heard the sound of a woman weeping.

"Misery. That's what you've got, you know, the pure

stuff. Anguish, loneliness, despair? They all come from this source." He sighed, tapping the box. "Hopelessness. Phew . . . don't I know about that, huh? My wife's off with another—another—ah, well, never mind. And it's not like everyone doesn't already know. Shouldn't be burdening . . . you . . ."

He gave a sad little laugh that broke Alcie's heart in two. He swiftly fitted the square shackles around the small wooden box and closed the clasp.

"Thank you, oh magnificent smitty—smithy!" Alcie said with a tiny smile.

"Stop, Alcestis," he said humbly. "I'm just a working god."

As Pandy had done before, Alcie impulsively rushed forward and kissed his cheek. Not to be outdone, Iole did the same.

Hephaestus just shook his head.

"You maidens are something else." He smiled.

With that he clambered back up on his chair and raised his terrible hammer high.

"Be good!"

With a swing and a clang, he and the anvil disappeared.

CHAPTER TEN

Inevitable

What *was* the word?

"In—" something, and it meant that something, some event, was bound to happen. No escaping it. Like the Fates had decreed it or Zeus had said it would be.

Pandy sat on the hard ground and let her brain just struggle awhile, trying to come up with the word. For the foreseeable future, she had nothing but time and was doing a great deal of thinking.

She reached her hand to her face, trying to wipe a speck of dust out of her eye, but was stopped short. The woman next to her in the line of prisoners was asleep, lying on the short chain linking their manacles, and Pandy didn't have the heart to wake her up.

In fact everyone was asleep except her, two guards watching the huddled group of prisoners, and the three guards sitting around a fire some distance away.

Inevitable!

"That's it," Pandy thought. It was inevitable that she and the boys would finally be caught. She just didn't think it would be this soon.

So, if it was absolutely inevitable, why was she still blaming herself? The gods themselves knew she had done everything possible to keep herself and the boys safe, and for the previous three days she'd been very successful. Since Athena had healed Amri's leg only the night before, and this morning there was no more than a light scab over flat skin, Pandy had rejoiced in the early light, certain that they would make much better time. But that certainty had ended only a few hours later.

At dawn they had begun their usual scurry alongside the road, keeping to the brush. But a large bare stretch had left them exposed. Amri heard the sound of clanking metal and heavy footsteps first, and Pandy had raced the boys to the nearest clump of rocks she saw up the hill. It was too small, and too late. Raiding parties, one after another, began passing back and forth on the trail below, leaving them unable to move a muscle.

Pandy and the boys had been pinned behind some rocks for hours, forced to crouch in painful and awkward positions, their bodies barely hidden. In the heat of midday, unable even to reach into her pouch for food or water, Pandy, drowsy herself, had watched the boys drift off to sleep, thankful that at least in slumber they wouldn't feel the terrible cramps in their legs and arms. But Ismailil, although unconscious, had apparently had enough and slowly extended his right leg out from behind the rocks, in plain sight of everyone on the road.

Pandy had woken to spears under her throat and the captains of two different raiding parties fighting over who was going to take the trio to Jbel Toubkal, the peak of the Atlas Mountains. Finally, it was agreed that the party heading toward the mountain peak would take them, provided that credit for the capture was given to the other. The manacles were slapped on, the chains were tightened, and the three new prisoners joined the back of the line.

The kidnappers hurriedly went through all of the trio's possessions, taking whatever interested them. They took a small ring out of Ismailil's ear and a cuff off Amri's wrist, which one soldier used to hold his hair. But when they examined Pandy's leather carrying pouch, they found it completely empty. Nothing. And it was now extremely tattered and stained. Not wanting to be bothered with such shabbiness, they hung it roughly back around her neck.

Her face betrayed nothing; where once she would have rolled her eyes or smirked, now she stared straight ahead and her mouth was a thin line of neutrality. But her brain was hurtling a kilometer a second, at once thanking the gods again for keeping the box, the shells, and the map safe and memorizing the face of the soldier who was starting to handle Ismailil harshly, swearing by the Great Bow of Artemis that if he hurt the little boy in any way, she would turn him to ashes right there on the spot. And she didn't care who noticed.

"Move when I say move! Understand? Say something, you little brat!"

"He doesn't speak," Pandy said, stepping as close to Ismailil as she could, her voice calm. "Neither of them does. I think it's shock."

The soldier spit on the ground in front of Ismailil and, giving the small boy a shove, walked to the front of the line. On a signal, the entire line began to move slowly up the road and deeper into the mountains. Fortunately, the guards had put Pandy in between the brothers, with Amri last in line, so when he stumbled for the third time, Pandy was able to carry him without tensing anyone else's chains. They walked until they could walk no more, then they walked farther.

The rest of the day seemed three times longer than any other Pandy had ever known.

There were no rest periods.

Finally, the prisoners were herded onto a sloping hillside and told to sit. Water-skins and flatbread were flung randomly into the crowd, where the prisoners scrabbled among each other for a bite or a drop, while the kidnappers below roasted meats over a blinding fire. At length, from exhaustion (and because they were warned that if they spoke to each other, their tongues would be removed), one by one they dropped off to sleep.

All except Pandy.

CHAPTER ELEVEN

Misery

Coming back up on deck, Alcie and Iole discovered the fog hanging just overhead with a few wisps beginning to curl around the mast poles and guard towers. Hiding themselves behind the closest tower, preparing to creep back across the deck, Alcie and Iole suddenly heard a commotion where the cook was serving evening meal.

Alcie poked her head out from behind the tower. At least fifty pirates, swords and knives at the ready, surrounded the cook.

"We wanted *meat* in the soup!" yelled Gaius, his sword closest to the cook's throat.

"Meat!" shouted a chorus of voices.

"Five gold coins he jumps in before we can throw him in!" muttered one pirate.

"You have a wager!" said another.

"I *put* meat in the soup!" pleaded the terrified cook.

"Then what's this?" another pirate snarled as he

stepped forward, forcing the cook to swallow a huge mouthful out of a bowl.

"Toss him in!"

"Oh, merciful Venus," said the cook, "that's for the little girl! The maiden who won't eat meat. I must have given you the wrong batch! But there's more—down below. Just let me—"

The cook began backing up toward the rail.

"Oh, we'll let you, Lucius," said Gaius gently, lowering his sword and tossing his arm cheerfully around the cook. "Certainly we'll let you."

With lightning speed, Gaius lifted the cook over his shoulders and tossed him into the sea.

"We'll let you swim back to Africa!" Gaius shouted as Lucius landed with a splash. "Now, men, to the real soup!"

With a roar, the pirates began moving toward the middle of the ship.

"Go!" Alcie said to Iole.

The two girls scuttled like mice, praying the fog would hide them. Skirting the railing, they raced against the approaching voices, slipping down the stairs, through the passageway, and into their cabin, only steps ahead of being seen by anyone.

Alcie threw the adamant-shackled box into her carrying pouch and flung herself on her pallet.

"Lemon rinds! I'm glad that's over."

"Uh . . . hello?" said Iole.

"What?"

"We're not done!"

"As if!"

"The book!" Iole all but shouted.

"Oh!" Alcie jumped off her pallet. "Right! The book! What are you doing just standing there? Let's go. Hey, bring your dad's sword, we might use it."

"I know how I'd *like* to use it," Iole mumbled, grabbing the sword and following Alcie.

Out of the cabin, Iole saw that Alcie's momentary eagerness had suddenly eased. She was softly knocking on Homer's door.

"Homer? It's Alcie. Please . . ."

"Go away."

"Hom—"

"I'm all right, just . . . leave me alone."

"Come on, Alcie," Iole said beside her. "I don't think he's going anywhere. Let's go get this thing while the captain is away. Okay?"

As Alcie nodded and started down the passageway, Iole saw on her friend's face everything that Alcie had tried so hard to keep from telling her: she truly cared for the oversized youth, and if Iole had read all the signs right, Homer cared for Alcie as well. For reasons she couldn't explain (even with her mighty brain), this thought made Iole smile, and she resolved not to pester Alcie further about her feelings for Homer.

Approaching the captain's cabin once more, they expected to hear a cacophony of shrieks and moans as arrows flew out of the room. But instead, when they poked their heads around the door, they saw Eros simply sitting on the open cover of the book, laughing and squealing, his bow off to one side.

Seeing them, Eros flew up and buzzed very close to Alcie's ear, then ran, laughing, straight across her forehead. Without thinking Iole raised her sword to hit him and came very close to chopping off Alcie's nose.

"Iole . . . stop!" said Alcie. "Let him go! Alpha, he's a god, and beta, I'll wager my ruby and pearl hairclip that he's not part of what goes in the box."

"Gods," said Iole, "I should have thought of that."

Eros flew by and tickled Iole's ear as he bolted out the doorway and up the passage.

"Now . . . the book. How do we capture . . . ?" said Alcie, as both turned their attention to the rows of teeth.

But the teeth were gone.

At least it looked that way from across the room. Iole scanned the inside rim of the book. It was smooth and even.

"That's weird," she said.

"Yes, and we're living such normal lives," said Alcie dryly.

They stared at what appeared to be a plain leather book cover with a few sheaves of papyrus still loosely bound inside. Finally Alcie reached out her hand and held the soft brown calfskin between her fingers.

"I think whatever enchantment the book had fallen under must have been lifted when we captured Misery," she said, pulling the book toward her.

"And the *Syracusa* is not rolling or shuddering anymore," affirmed Iole.

"Excellent!" said Alcie.

Slowly, she loosened the red cords binding the letters to the cover. Alcie and Iole spread several of the letters—there were about thirty or so that had not been turned into Eros's arrows—out in front of them. Taking one apiece, they unfolded the yellowed parchment.

"Oh!" Iole gasped slightly as a long strand of beautiful chestnut-colored hair fell out of the letter in her hand.

"Totally gross or kinda beautiful . . . I can't decide," said Alcie, holding up the hair. "Are these all from the same woman?"

"They've got to be," said Iole, lighting a nearby oil lamp.

"These have a lot of gray in them, though," Alcie said, examining other letters. "Look, this hair isn't stringy and ashy, and the words on this letter aren't fading away like before."

"That was probably because of the spell cast by the lesser evil of Misery . . . like the teeth on the book," said Iole.

"Look at the signature," said Alcie, glancing from letter to letter. "It's never the same way twice."

They both looked down toward the bottom of their pages.

"Yours for eternity, Latona."

"Your beloved, Latona."

"Yours in loneliness, Latona."

"Your wretched Latona."

"Figs, listen to this," said Alcie, and she read aloud from the letter in her hand.

Honored Husband,

These past weeks have been as a lifetime to me, and I pray each day for your safe return. The new moon which brings you home again cannot wax soon enough. Why do you not write? You must know how lonely your absence has made me. You must pass other ships which could deliver a letter, a note to me, do you not? Spare me my loneliness.

In eros, Latona

"What about this?" said Iole. "Um . . . *'My love'* . . . *'missing you'* . . . okay, listen to this . . ."

. . . this unease which has gripped my heart will not cease. Today I passed the harbor and thought my eyes beheld your sails. My heart leapt high, but I was deceived. Poseidon is taunting me. My grief at your absence is killing me surely. How I wish you would write.

Awaiting, Latona

With each letter they unfolded, the girls read of the woman's struggle with her crushing loneliness and despair. She had been the wife of the captain of the ship, left alone for months (sometimes years, they read) at a time. She'd had a child, a boy, who'd grown to manhood without a father's love.

. . . how he favors you, dearest . . . would that you were here to see it . . .

She'd managed a house and servants, raised her child, and lived out her entire life absolutely alone; forever waiting for her husband's return. The letters began to become more desperate and pleading, until finally they dissolved into incoherent ramblings.

"Oh . . . no . . . ," said Alcie, reading one of the few remaining letters, strands of pure gray in her hands.

"What? What is it?"

Alcie lifted her head up and looked at her friend. Iole's eyes widened slightly and her heart *thuh-rump*ed a little in her chest. Alcie had a tear coursing down her cheek.

"Listen," she said, the words sticking in her throat.

Sir,

With regret we must inform you that your wife has crossed the river Styx. We believe her death, by no other hand than her own, was swift and painless. Your son, now a youth of 14, is well and is being cared for by the graciousness of the city. All rites and ceremonies for your wife have been prepared and her passage to the Elysian Fields has been assured.

City High Council

"Hounds of Hades," said Iole, "she killed herself."

"Because she was so lonely. Because of Misery. I'm sure of it."

Suddenly, something directly over Iole's shoulder caught Alcie's attention: a small stuffed bear made of green and bright blue fabric was lying at the end of the captain's sleeping cot. Next to it was a stuffed rabbit skin with glass eyes and a pink nose. On the floor was a smooth, round piece of wood with bells and strange black symbols all over it. She glanced to her right and spotted a tiny drum of some exotic kind and a small white toy horse with wings on its back, barely visible behind a decorative fabric draping. And the crates that had been covered by the cloth Alcie had used to capture Misery were each full to the brim with more toys.

"Hey, why are there toys—?" she started, but she had no time to finish her sentence.

There was a sudden, loud noise in the outer passageway. Someone was coming, with heavy footsteps.

Madly, Alcie tried to gather the letters together and place them back between the covers of the book, while Iole ran about pulling letter-arrows out of the walls. But in her rush she and Iole collided coming around the corner of the table, succeeding only in scattering everything further around the room. They heard the footsteps stop and knew that someone, someone big, was standing in the doorway. Alcie and Iole both turned around sheepishly and, looking up, locked eyes with the captain.

He stared hard at the girls for a moment and then he looked at the mess strewn all over his cabin floor. At his sides, his hands were balled in tight fists.

The captain cleared his throat, and Alcie's eyes instantly met his once again. She suddenly knew what it was like to watch a volcano about to explode. The captain was trying to hold himself back, but she felt sure that he wanted them dead on the spot.

"If I could," he began slowly, "I would tie both of you

to the top of the mainsail and let the seabirds feast on your eyes."

"But—," Alcie began, but Iole pinched her hard on the arm.

"Again with the pinching," Alcie muttered.

"How do you *dare!*" the captain said, his voice building in intensity. "I warned you—I ordered you. Prying into my personal property, desecrating my possessions, is something I will not *tolerate!*"

"Sir . . . Captain . . . sir," said Alcie, "we didn't have a choice. Really, we didn't. I'm *so* not kidding. This book was already on the floor underneath the table. Your wife's letters were being turned into arrows by Eros, and he was shooting them at us! Look!"

And she pointed to the walls of the cabin and then to the walls of the corridor.

"My wife's letters . . . ?" His voice fell away as he looked around the room.

"We had to defend ourselves, sir!" said Iole.

"No, you didn't!" the captain cried. "By Zeus! You could have walked away. You could have come to find me! This is none of your business!"

"Grape skins . . . that's so not true," said Alcie, then quickly went on. "I can explain. I mean, can I explain? 'Cause I can explain—everything."

"Explain? Explain your snooping in my quarters? Well, go ahead. This I must hear."

"Okay," said Alcie, stooping to pick up the letters.

"Don't touch anything else!" cried the captain. "Don't even move or I will be only too happy to run a sword through each of you."

"Um . . . okay," said Alcie.

"Start talking, maiden."

Quickly and concisely, Alcie told of the box, the school project, Pandy's trip to Olympus, and the quest for the great and lesser evils. She explained exactly why she and her friends had been on the *Peacock*, their adventures in Egypt, the ride in Apollo's Sun Chariot, Pandy's fall, and the crash landing. But Alcie made certain to stress how important it was that the tiny figure of a woman—"I think it was probably the spirit of your wife," she interrupted herself—was captured and placed in the box. She and Iole were certain that the woman-spirit was the hiding place of a lesser evil.

"It's Misery," she sidetracked again.

She explained that they both thought the answer might be found in the letters, which is the only reason they read them.

". . . and that's when we read about your wife killing herself. And then you came in . . . and then we . . . stopped," she finished.

The captain stared blankly at each of the girls in turn.

"I told Homer not to touch that map. It looks like I have many snoops aboard my ship."

"He didn't mean to, sir," said Iole. "He wasn't snooping. The chart had come loose and the book of your wife's letters fell out. He was trying to put it back and that's when it bit him."

The captain looked at her, eyebrows raised.

"Before we got the spirit of your wife in the box," Iole continued, "the book had rows of sharp teeth. But please don't blame Homer."

"And I thought I had hidden it so carefully," he said, gazing without really looking around his cabin. "Shameful thing."

He turned back to the girls.

"You are mistaken in one thing, Alcie."

"Figures," she said.

The captain stooped to pick up several of the unfolded letters; he looked solemnly at the words before him, then held the letters to his heart.

"These are not my wife's letters," the captain said.

"They aren't?" Iole asked.

"No," he replied. "Latona was my mother."

The girls stood very still.

"Then," Iole said at last, "you were the boy in the letter. You never knew your father?"

"Never *knew* him?" the captain said with a sneer. "I never *met* him."

He sat down heavily at the table, leaving Alcie and Iole standing, feeling somewhat helpless.

"My mother would show me a marble bust of my father . . . the great man of the sea!" he began. "Or she'd point to a statue of him in our garden and tell me what a fine man he was. And each day, as I grew up, my mother became more and more lonely. And I became more and more angry. He sent us money . . . but wouldn't even write to her. Finally, I came home from the academy one day and the house servants gathered around and told me what had happened. I was immediately taken from my home to the one place I swore I would never go—aboard a ship. I wanted to be nothing like my father. But the City High Council told me they were under orders!"

"Orders?" said Iole. "Who was left to give orders?"

"Who indeed?" he said.

The captain paused for a long moment. "It's as if," Alcie thought, "he's trying to decide just how much he can or should tell."

The captain rose and walked to his chest of private possessions. He lifted the heavy lid and took out a large rectangular case made from a metal that glowed with a faint light blue. He set the case on the table and placed his hand on the clasp, looking at the girls once more.

"Wondrous Aphrodite was and is now in charge of my life. One night, after I'd been at sea only a few weeks, I had a strange urge to go up on deck while everyone slept. Aphrodite the Beautiful rose from the water on

117 ▣

the back of a mighty two-tailed fish, telling me *she* had set me to work on the ship and that I would ultimately become its captain, living out the rest of my days alone and at sea. No man in my lineage would ever again have the chance to make anyone as lonely as my father had made my mother. This was the decree of the Goddess of Love. I would never marry, never know the company of a caring woman, never have a family, and I would never live away from a ship."

He paused and took a deep breath.

"And the same fate . . . my enduring punishment for the sins of a loveless, self-centered father . . . would befall my sons."

"Oranges," said Alcie. "That's so horrible. I mean— wait! What?"

"Excuse me?" said Iole.

"How can you have sons if you can't have a family?" said Alcie.

The captain smiled weakly, as if he alone knew the answer to the saddest question ever asked, and lifted up the lid of the case, revealing a soft white light and a faint sound, like the cooing of doves. Inside, surrounded by many folds of deep purple silk, was a gleaming white egg the size of a large melon.

"Grape seeds, that's some first meal," Alcie said, then slapped her hand over her mouth.

The captain stared blankly at Alcie for a moment,

then began to laugh very hard and very quietly, almost doubling over.

"Never before have I laughed about my dilemma," he said at last, wiping his eyes. Then he waved his hand across the case. "Maidens, this is . . . or will someday be . . . my son."

The captain lifted the egg out of the case and held it up to the light of an oil lamp. Inside, the girls could see the faintest outline of a tiny, tightly curled human form.

Alcie looked around again; now the toys made sense. There was baby stuff everywhere! But the girls had been so busy focusing on Misery that they hadn't noticed. The top shelf of a bookcase was filled with tiny clothes made of the finest cotton and soft, fur-lined leather infant booties. A small Egyptian reed basket lined with a thin Chinese silk mattress and covered with a fine Persian linen blanket lay at the foot of the captain's pallet. Above this, a crude mobile was nailed into the ceiling. Dangling from it were painted papyrus horses, dryads, lightning bolts, musical instruments, and fishes. There were odd toys and colorful baby clothes from all over the known world peeking out of strange hiding places about the room.

"Wait a tick on the sundial, if you please!" cried Alcie. "This is the *Syracusa*! The *Peacock* was destroyed! How did everything from that ship get *here*?"

"Nothing can change what the gods decree," the

captain said. "When I was spared by the pirates and given the helm of this ship, they brought me down here. Aphrodite, I'm certain, put everything back in its place. This cabin is an exact duplicate of my old cabin on the *Peacock*."

Their attention was drawn back to the cooing coming from within the folds of silk.

"What's that sound?" asked Iole.

"The dove is Aphrodite's protected bird. I think those sounds are keeping my son safe in some way . . . perhaps even imparting knowledge to him. Nourishing him."

He put the egg gingerly back in the box.

"Aphrodite told me that I should have an heir," the captain said, "who will also have an heir, and so forth, and so the line will continue. I had no idea what she was talking about until one night, several months ago, Aphrodite in a dream gave me instructions to visit a particular market stall the next time I put in to the port at Athens. The vendor handed me this box and refused to take even a single drachma. He only repeated the phrase 'nine moons' over and over. When I got back to the *Peacock* and opened the box, I found this egg and the book of my mother's letters to my father."

He sighed deeply.

"I used to pray every day to Aphrodite to release me from this curse," he continued. "Now I simply pray to all the gods to be able to raise my son well. I keep the egg close so I can tend to it, but I didn't want to look at my mother's letters, so I hid the book where I thought it would be safe and forgotten, long before Pandora opened the box. I had no way of knowing that it had since become a dangerous, enchanted thing. It makes perfect sense, though, that the pure source of Misery would find a home within it. I know it lived within my mother while she was still alive."

"Do you think it was your mother's spirit we put in the box?" asked Iole.

"No," he replied. "Aphrodite has assured me that my mother's soul is happy in the Elysian Fields. I think it was Misery in the shape of my mother."

There was silence as they all pondered the effect Misery could have.

"Doesn't seem like a 'lesser' evil to me," said Iole.

"So your son is gonna have an egg, too?" said Alcie.

"Um . . . can we help you clean all of this up?" asked Iole quickly.

"No, but thank you . . . I shall attend to it myself," the captain replied, looking at the letters everywhere. "I think I'll do a little reading."

CHAPTER TWELVE

Blackmail

Hera returned to her rooms from raiding the food cupboards, two oversized bowls of ambrosia in her hands. She had nothing for Dido; she didn't even so much as glance in his direction.

Demeter was only seconds behind, carrying goblets of nectar and two large spoons.

"Oh," she giggled, "I feel like a mortal at one of those chic Roman Somnus parties where all the girls get together and paint their nails and give each other makeovers and gossip all night . . . Where's the dog?"

"Huh?" said Hera, whirling about.

"Where's the dog?"

"Probably hiding," Hera said.

"No," said Demeter, walking into the corner, gazing under the divan. "He's not here."

"What do you mean, he's *not* here?" shrieked Hera.

"The corner is still warm," Demeter said, feeling the

stones, "and there's a trail of something sticky leading out onto your balcony."

"Looks like sandal prints . . . in blood," said Hera, following the prints outside.

The dark red trail led across Hera's balcony, with one print on the far railing, but it didn't continue on the balconies of the adjoining apartments belonging to Hermes, Artemis, and Apollo. It was only looking at the far end of the wing that Hera saw a tiny speck of red dot the railing of the corner apartment.

"Ares," Hera muttered.

"Oh no," Demeter whispered. "How do you think he found out?"

"The brat," Hera spat, moving inside. "She prayed to him. I heard her. Clever girl. I just didn't think he would be so bold . . . but he's left me his signature trail."

"What are you going to do?"

"Keep the nectar cold," Hera said, clomping through the entryway. "This won't take long."

Hera strode down the long hallway, passing fountains and gardens. Halfway to Ares' rooms, she nearly plowed into Artemis, arriving fresh from a hunt.

"Hey!" yelled Artemis. "Watch where you're going!"

"Sorry, dear," Hera said, acting nonchalant, but continuing on. "Oh my, you look all spent. You should take a nap . . . and definitely a bath. If you'll excuse me."

Hera pretended to examine an exotic floral

arrangement on the far side of the hall until Artemis entered her own apartments. Then she wound her way around several bushes and placed herself squarely in Ares' entryway. At the sight of her, Dido, lying on a low fur pallet, a huge bowl of choice meats half eaten in front of him, immediately began to growl.

"Hush now," came a gravelly voice from a chair in the corner of the room. "Rest."

Immediately, Dido fell asleep.

"You have something of mine," Hera said, regaining her composure.

"You *had* something of hers," Ares replied.

"I'd like it back."

"I'm glad to see you, at least, are remaining well fed," said Ares, ignoring her comment.

Hera gazed at Ares. She noticed his helmet, on a table by his side, knowing full well that Ares removed it only when he wanted to be particularly imposing.

"I have to eat," she replied, calmly ignoring the battle scars that covered his face (some of which bled afresh eternally) and his yellow eyes, narrowed into slits.

"So does the dog," Ares said. "You mistreated my protected animal and I'm not going to stand by and—"

"Blah, blah. I feed him—"

"I won't argue," Ares interrupted. "Now go away or I'll let it slip to Zeus that he's here and who brought him. Which I might do anyway."

Hera walked toward Ares, her voice set at a purr.

"And what exactly will you say?"

"That I was visiting Aphrodite; her apartments are not far from yours. I heard a yelp and I came to check it out. I found the dog dirty, panicked, and starving, which he was. It won't take Zeus long to put alpha and beta together."

"Fine," Hera said, looking directly into Ares' eyes. "Tell him your theories now that you've revealed them to me, wonderful strategist that you are. And when he asks me about it, I will tell him that I know how precious the animal is to Pandora and that I took him only out of love for the child. That this quest is too dangerous for such a helpless animal . . . that I only took him to keep him safe until, and if, she returns. That it is *I* who was protecting him. Now, whom do you think Zeus will believe?"

Ares stared at Hera for a moment.

"Me," he said quietly. "And the dog."

At a snap of his fingers, Dido woke and, looking at Hera, began to speak.

"You are one nasty lady."

Hera gasped and Ares chuckled.

"You snatched me out of the palace of Cleopatra," Dido began, "when my mistress was distracted. You trapped me, threw a chain around my neck, and dragged me across the sky. Just to make Pandy miserable and lead her off-track. Don't think she doesn't know. And now you have to beat up on a *dog*? You are one nasty—"

Ares snapped again and Dido was silent.

"Even so," Hera said after a moment, only the slightest hint of doubt in her voice, "Zeus won't touch me."

"Go away and let me think of what you can do to keep me from telling him."

Defiantly Hera strode toward the entryway and was almost out when she spun on her heel.

"You're not the boss of me!"

Ares stared at her.

"Fine, keep the mutt!"

Ares continued to stare.

"Zeus hates you, you know. He hates that you're actually a coward in battle, hates that you run screaming in pain every time you get so much as a hangnail. Would love to disown you and kick you off the mountain."

Ares stared, then sighed.

"Yes, but he knows my word is good."

He paused.

"Interesting, isn't it? He hates me but delights in hurting you. I'll take the deal I have, because at least it's honest. The dog stays here, Mother."

CHAPTER THIRTEEN
Poison Pen

"We saw him every day on the *Peacock* . . . just talking to himself," Iole said, skirting a few letter-arrows sticking out of the walls farther down the passageway. "Now here, when we go up on deck, he just wanders over to the railing and . . . at least, I thought he was talking to himself. Can you believe he prays to all the gods—every day! That's a lot of praying."

"We've been doing a lot of praying too, you know," Alcie countered.

"Yes, but not to *everyone*," Iole said.

"He must ask Athena for wisdom and Apollo for the ability to heal . . . you know, if his little boy ever gets sick or something," said Alcie.

"I'll bet he asks Hermes to make his little boy clever and Artemis to protect him," said Iole.

"I'm just wondering what he prays to Hera for," said Alcie.

At the mention of Hera's name, the girls were silent. They rounded the corner of the passageway and were almost to their cabin when Iole halted.

"Look," she said, pointing across the corridor.

The door to Homer's cabin was slightly ajar and a small scrap of papyrus was just visible underneath.

Alcie knocked softly on the old, worn wood. There was no answer from inside, so she gently opened the door.

Homer sat on the end of his sleeping pallet, eyes closed and a peaceful smile on his face. He was rubbing his wounded hand with a piece of faded pink cloth, softly humming to himself. Beside him on the cot lay two tidy stacks of papyrus sheets, each about one centimeter high, and a quill pen, its feathers bent and smashed at odd angles.

"Homer?" said Alcie. "Are you all right?"

Homer opened his eyes as the two girls cautiously stepped into his cabin.

"Hi," he said, his voice sounding old and tired. He took the pink fabric away from his bite.

"Homer! Your hand!" Iole gasped.

"What?" said Alcie.

Homer held up his hand; the bite wound was completely healed.

"Well . . . it was the other hand, then," said Alcie.

Homer looked at her and held up his other palm.

Perfect. A little rough, a few calluses, but otherwise, both hands were just fine.

"I'm sorry I left you," Homer began, "but I knew I would just mess things up. After that thing bit me, I started feeling terrible. So sad. Like, I was feeling sad for everyone else. I had taken all the sadness that there ever was or ever would be into myself."

"Misery?" asked Iole.

"Yeah! That's it," he answered. "And so I came back here. I thought about going up on deck, but the only thing I could think of to do there was to jump overboard. Then I saw my quill and my papyrus and, like, I just started writing."

He looked at the stack of papyrus beside him on the cot and pointed to an empty flask of ink that had rolled into one corner of the cabin.

"This stuff started coming out of me . . . ," he continued.

"By the bank of the eddying river, clear voiced, the swan alighting sings of Apollo to the beating of his own wings . . ."

Alcie had picked up the stray piece of papyrus from underneath the door. She read the scribbled lines of poetry with the utmost sincerity, almost reverence, but Homer bolted off the cot and tore it out of her hands.

"What? It's good! It's really good," she said as he turned his back on her.

"It's private," he said. He stayed with his back to the girls for a moment. Finally, he turned around.

"I was writing about things I had never felt before," he said. "Then, like, all at once, it started getting weaker and weaker. I mean, that feeling . . . it wasn't gone immediately, but it was leaving me. And my hand was healing. It was really neat—but I still needed to write."

"You were poisoned," said Iole flatly.

"Huh?" Homer said.

"The lesser evil that you found in the book was Misery," said Alcie. "We've got it in a box with adamant shackles around it—oh, and you missed seeing Hephaestus—and when we captured Misery, the teeth on the book disappeared; that's probably when your hand healed up and you started feeling better."

"You wrote so much!" said Iole, now standing next to the pallet, gazing at the two stacks.

"It's the only thing I could think of. I'm named after my great-great-great-great—there are a lot them—great-great-grandfather. I've always only wanted to be a poet like him," he answered.

"Gods," Iole spoke with reverence, "are you related to *that* Homer?"

"On my mother's side."

"Staggering!"

"Cantaloupes!"

"Why are there two stacks?" asked Iole.

"These are the things I wrote when I was feeling depressed," he said, pointing to one stack. "And this is what I wrote when the feeling went away." He held the other stack in his hand. "But if you say I was poisoned, then maybe I didn't really write them at all . . . maybe it was just the poison working through me."

Suddenly, Iole had the feeling there was much more to Homer than a wide set of shoulders, slightly limited vocabulary, and a deep affection for Alcie.

"Will you read us something . . . please?" she asked.

"Do you promise you, like, won't laugh?" he asked.

"We so do," said Alcie.

"Um, okay," he said, flipping through the stack of poems he'd written under the influence of Misery. "Okay, this is about one friend who betrays another—"

"Ouch," said Alcie.

He revealed, in perfectly phrased stanzas and stunning, piercingly beautiful words, the bitter pain felt when one loses a treasured friendship.

"And it kinda, like, goes on from there," he said after reading a bit.

There was a full thirty-second pause. Homer cast his eyes downward.

"Is it that horri—?" he began.

"Yes, yes," said Iole, "I think it's justifiable now. After

my dad, Pandy, Pandy's dad, Alcie, Dido, Athena, Hermes, Hephaestus, and the High Priestesses of Delphi, you are, officially and without sanction, the coolest person I know."

Alcie just gaped at the tall boy whose head almost bumped against the ceiling.

"And I thought the poem you wrote for *me* was good!"

Homer's smile lit up the cabin.

"Beauty from grief!" Iole was now mumbling to herself. "Who knew? Beauty from grief!"

"Homie—er," Alcie said, "read just one more . . . please?"

"Okay," he said, picking up a piece of papyrus from the other stack. "This one is a hymn to Aphrodite."

After his reading, there was another full thirty-second pause.

"That's better than the first stack," Iole said, as if in a trance. "Homer, I surmise that you needn't worry that it was only the poison. First of all, you wrote a wonderful poem for Alcie way back in Egypt, certainly not under the influence of Misery. And you wrote a stack of amazing things after Misery was out of your system. My hypothesis is that Misery opened up a creative channel for you and that your writing will only evolve!"

"Cool."

"Indubitably."

"I want to take some of your poems and hymns to school for the next big Gods project, if there is one," Alcie said. "If Pandy had found these, she never would have messed up like she did."

"If she hadn't messed up, I guess I never would have written this stuff," he replied.

"He's right!" said Iole. "And you two would never have . . . met . . . nothing, never mind. Way to go, Pandy! Wherever you are."

They were all jolted from their momentary happiness by a tremendous shout from the deck.

"Land! Land ahead!"

CHAPTER FOURTEEN
Oh, Heavens!

From the moment Pandy and the boys had been captured, they had been forced to walk, on a gentle but steady incline, from sunrise to sundown each day, with only a short break for mid-meal. Absolute silence was demanded among the captives. Consulting her diary or calling her father at night was out of the question: that would have been downright stupid. But Pandy knew that her father would be out of his mind with worry; she'd never gone so long without letting him know she was okay.

During the first few days, Pandy tapped into reserves of strength (for which she was constantly thanking the gods) in order to carry Amri during times when the little boy became just too tired. Small rest periods came when one raiding party met another and the captains conferred about road conditions, mountain weather, and which towns were going to be plundered next. Or when a prisoner was cut from the line and left on the road.

Sixteen days later, Pandy realized that the entire group could go no farther: the black wall was directly in front of them, blocking the main road, stretching endlessly off to each side and as high above them as they could see. The bottom of the whole mass was hovering less than half a meter off the ground. And, almost indiscernibly, it was creeping toward them.

She and the boys had been subsisting on the tiny rations: very little water and even less food. So, although she had managed once in a while to secretly dip her hands into her pouch and pull out a few dried figs or apricots, she was not at all surprised to find herself hallucinating.

She could see . . . shapes. Hundreds of them.

Staring at the blackness, her brain tricked her eyes into thinking she saw large gray masses on the other side, quite bright, just floating. Suspended. Spheres, most of them, of every size imaginable, suspended in a black soup.

"What are they?" asked Ismailil.

"Oh, good," Pandy thought, slightly dizzy from hunger, "the boys can see them too." It was comforting to know she wasn't the only one losing her mind.

She hadn't time to come up with a good lie for the brothers.

"On your bellies!" came the order from the front, passed in a shout back along the line.

The entire group was being forced to the ground. Those who didn't comply quickly enough had their legs flung out from under them by the flat edges of well-swung swords.

Guards were checking the line to make certain everyone was lying on their stomachs, as flat as possible. Then the captain stood at the midpoint so that all could hear.

"You have five days on your bellies, more or less. Keep your noses to the ground. I repeat, do not lift your heads. Don't touch anything except the road you crawl upon. Only a few of us will accompany you, but we're used to what lies ahead, so if anyone gets the bright idea to attempt an escape, we'll hunt you down and force you to stand."

A truly nasty laugh ran through the kidnappers.

"It's been . . . a pleasure. Move!"

Slowly, the line began to inch forward as the prisoners actually began to crawl into the space *underneath* the black wall. One woman close to the head of the line began screaming madly. There was a thud and the screaming stopped, but the line kept moving. Pandy kept her head low, eyes, hands, stomach, and legs on the dirt, which was still cold from the previous night. A sudden spasm of humiliation shook her: this was disgusting and degrading, being made to crawl like a beast. From out of nowhere, a flash of anger lit up her brain, but she squelched it as soon as she felt tension in the chain behind her. Amri was desperately trying to back away from the wall.

"I'm scared." He almost choked on his tears.

Pandy realized these were the first words she'd heard from the little boy. Her mind went to that strange, responsible place. "Well, I'm not! This is, like, so neat. We can pretend we're snakes! Or alligators! And it's only for five days. Okay, I'm gonna be a two-headed green snake with black and yellow spots, slithering over the ground looking for mice. Amri, what are you going to be?"

Less than three months ago, she would have thought she sounded like the biggest, geekiest loser plebe in the known world. Now it was a matter of survival.

The back of the line was now moving into the very small space between the ground and the bottom of the black wall. The air was thick and brown with so much dust; Pandy could see only a meter in any direction. Escape? To where? Plus, she caught sight through the haze of the tiny, reddish men with short spears corralling the prisoners.

"This is dumb. A snake can't have two heads," Ismailil called ahead of her.

"Well, I do," Pandy said. "Amri, what kind of animal are you?"

"Uh," his little voice trembled, "I can't see!"

"You don't have to. Just follow me. Now come on, what kind of animal are you?"

"I'm a brown lizard with gold stripes," said Ismailil.

"Very, very cool," Pandy said. "Amri?"

"I'm a snake too, but I'm bigger than you and I have a blue nose and I'm going to pretend that I'm always hunting you and I'm right behind you trying to gobble you up."

"Well, let's see if you can!"

And they were underneath.

Pandy kept her eyes shut against the polluted air, trying to breath through her teeth.

"You know what I like best about my snake?" she asked, putting a hiss in her voice. "I can slither with my eyes closed 'cause I have super smell capability."

"Me too," said Amri.

"I'm a lizard," replied Ismailil.

"Close enough," Pandy said.

But after an hour of struggling on the hard ground, moving forward only several hundred meters, Pandy and the boys abandoned the game in favor of silence, concentrating on how best to keep from shredding the skin on their arms and legs. Five more days of this, Pandy thought, and there would be no flesh left on any of them.

Suddenly, Pandy heard a tiny *whoosh* off to her right,

followed by a frantic squawk. Then her right arm brushed against something lying on the ground. Instinctively opening her eyes, she saw it was a fledgling bird. She reached to lift it gently out of Amri's path when the bird gave a feeble, almost soundless chirp and beat its wings against the earth, pushing itself farther off the road.

"What's that?" asked Ismailil.

"Nothing! Just a bird that got . . . um . . . no biggie," Pandy said. "Keep your eyes closed, okay?"

As the bird hobbled away, her eye caught something else off to the side: three more fledglings wandering in the dirt, the dense air around them making it difficult to fly. Then Pandy spied the mother, much larger and farther off, frantically screeching at something close overhead in the blackness. Pandy looked up and sharply gulped a lungful of thick, dusty air.

"What?" Ismailil asked.

"Uh . . . oh . . . I was hissing," Pandy lied, staring into the void.

"*Hisssss*," Amri said.

"Oh . . . hiss," said Ismailil, moving on.

In the blackness hanging above the earth, its wings beating furiously, a fifth fledgling was trapped. The mother bird extended her neck as far as she could, not daring to poke through the bottom of the void. Without warning, another fledgling lifted off the ground and flew close . . . too close. In a split second, the little bird pierced the bottom of the void and was sucked through the thin membrane with a soft *whoosh*. The mother bird now went mad. The first baby, eyes closed, wings barely moving, was floating on its side, and the second was thrashing wildly. The mother bird began pecking at the void, trying to reach her children. Extending her neck too high, she poked through and almost reached one fledgling, but the suction on the other side was too much and her body was being lifted off the ground. With a *whoosh,* she was pulled through. Pandy craned her neck to keep watching as the line continued to move and saw the two fledglings, quite still, and the mother, moving slightly, suspended close to the bottom. A large spherical shape softly bumped one fledgling in the moments that Pandy stared, sending it floating off in another direction.

Pandy felt as if she was going to be sick. "There's no air up there," she whispered.

Suddenly, clearly, the enormity of the horror came rushing in on Pandy.

The black void overhead was the heavens.

And the heavens were falling.

But why? How? Her uncle was supposed to be holding them up . . . for eternity. And if he wasn't doing that, if something had happened, then the heavens . . . where they weren't being held up, were . . . oh, Zeus! . . . were sagging. She flashed on her pallet linens at home: when she had crawled under them as a little girl to make a tent, the circle of linen closest to her always settled itself first, then spread like a wave in all directions.

Pandy looked up into an enormous black void. The heavens were slightly less than a meter from the surface of the earth, almost certainly spreading out in a great circular wave. The heaviness of the air in the thin layer between the heavens and the earth, the dust, and . . . whatever . . . were the only things that kept the earth from being completely smothered. Iole would know the precise reason, Pandy was certain, but she wasn't here to ask. But it meant that if the heavens continued to fall, soon the entire earth would have less than half a meter in which to live. She then realized that the spherical objects, the large gray masses very close now . . . were stars. The constellations, so beautiful in their original forms, were now being compacted as they fell down-ward. Some were being jumbled and mixed together, crashing into each other, completely out of order. She thought she could make out the crab . . . but then again, it might have been the big bear, or the archer, or a bunch of big gray rocks.

And why wasn't it pitch-black? They were so far underneath the heavens, she shouldn't have been able to see anything. Twisting around, she looked back far and high. She spotted a tiny glowing orb moving slowly, almost imperceptibly, above. The powerful sun was breaking through the darkness and giving the stars a glow that dimly lit up the thin crawlspace. Apollo was driving his chariot in the area of the sky not yet being compressed. Was he moving it slower, she wondered, or would the days become incredibly short? What would happen to the sun if the heavens covered the earth?

She closed her eyes and shook off those thoughts. If they were going to be on their stomachs for only five days, then there was fresh air and open space on the other side. She just had to keep the boys calm and moving that long. She would figure out the rest as it came.

Several hours later, the line was stopped; Pandy discovered this by plowing right into Ismailil. Amri stopped when Pandy slowed him with her hand.

"Can we sit up?" he asked.

"NO!" Pandy cried. "I mean, snakes can't sit."

"I'm tired of that game," Ismailil said.

"Okay, we won't play one for a while. Let's just stay down and see what happens."

Two of the tiny reddish men, able to negotiate the crawlspace easily, were scuttling alongside the line, tossing crusts of bread and squirting water from a skin into the open mouths of the prisoners with unerring accuracy.

"Please," Pandy begged, "just a little more for the boys?"

The reddish man with the flatbread just laughed and crawled back up the line, but the other, with the skin, took pity and gave each boy another squirt of water.

The brothers were strangely quiet during the rest break; both were on their backs staring straight up, their eyes darting from one point to another. There were many other things that had gotten caught in the void. Bushes and small trees hovered, pinecones floated, a rabbit hung suspended, a fox was stilled in midstride, and there were many, many birds. Someone had lost a sandal, someone else lost a cloak, and there were bits of flatbread scattered everywhere. She knew the boys must have been frightened, certainly curious, but Pandy didn't dare tell them what she suspected, so the three of them remained silent.

For three days they wriggled along. They had no way of gauging the time except when the stars began to dim even further. They rested, ate, and slept when they were told to. Pandy spoke little, only to comfort the boys, but she thought a great deal. What would Atlas be like? Would he respect the fact that she was his niece? Would he help her find Laziness?

Then on the afternoon of the third day, making their way over a smooth, well-worn stretch of road, Pandy was daydreaming about her favorite food: honeyed apricot-and-blood-orange cakes drizzled with sweet cream, when she heard a *whoosh* followed by a high-pitched scream.

The woman ahead of Ismailil had managed to slip her narrow wrist through her manacle and, still moving with the line, had tried to work her foot out of the adamant bond on her ankle. But in her struggle to escape, she had lifted her body off the ground to such an extent that her long black hair had been sucked into the void. Now her entire head was slowly being absorbed into the blackness as she shrieked and struggled wildly. Shouts went up the line as her torso began to be pulled upward, her mouth now gulping for air in the blackness. Several reddish men rushed in to pull her back to earth, but it was too late: with a final *pop*, her bound foot disappeared, the attached chain disappearing as it lifted higher . . .

. . . taking Ismailil's arm with it.

Ismailil was too stunned at first to make a sound, then when he realized *he* was about to be sucked up, he yelled and scrambled backward, clinging to Pandy.

The small reddish men were still pulling the chain attached to the woman when the right arm of one of the little men entered the void. Being so small and with nothing to anchor him, the creature was trapped in an instant. Ismailil was now being lifted off the ground. Pandy grabbed him by the waist but the force of the suction was like nothing she'd ever felt. He clawed at her, his eyes glazed over in terror. Then, with a horrible *whoosh,* his head disappeared. Now Pandy was being lifted as, with another *whoosh,* the second reddish man was sucked into the blackness. Ismailil was almost gone. Pandy stretched her body full out; sticking her hand into the void she grabbed the little boy's shoulder. Feeling an unknown strength surging through her body, she was just on the verge of pulling him back from certain death when she heard a loud *WHOOSH*, and then absolute silence.

She was floating. Completely weightless. Her limbs wafted to and fro.

And . . . she couldn't breathe.

Ismailil was still struggling; the woman who had tried to escape was barely moving; and Pandy, for several seconds, just took in the vastness of the heavens around her. Gods, she thought . . . it was so incredibly beautiful! There was a huge, strange sphere with a ring around it just overhead, and several other constellations were only centimeters away. She could have reached out and touched them, but the pressure on her lungs was now distracting her. What little air she still had in her body was fighting mercilessly to get out. Oddly, with her mind on complete overload, she didn't panic; she just stared back down at the ground, so close and so far. She saw the faces of the prisoners ahead of them in line, mouths wide open. She saw Amri's little hand poking through the thin membrane as the chain attaching them was drawn higher and despaired that he, too, was going to die.

Then her bottom hit something hard. Looking behind her, she realized that she'd hit one of the stars in the constellation Gemini, named after the triplets who founded the great city of Rome: Romulus, Remus, and Ralph. The force of her bump had sent Ralph careening off in a completely different direction.

"Ooops," she thought. She had an insane desire to giggle, but there was no air in her brain and she started to pass out.

Just as she was about to lose consciousness, she felt a sharp yank on her right leg and her body began to move as if she were being pulled through water. She looked down and saw three of the large men, lying on the ground at angles, pulling with all their might on the chain that linked the prisoners. Amri was already back on the ground, his eyes closed, gasping. Then, with an explosion of sound that almost burst her eardrums, Pandy was pulled out of the void. She lay with her eyes closed, feeling a sharp pain in her shoulder where she'd landed, gulping air, when suddenly Ismailil landed directly on top of her, unconscious. This forced Pandy's eyes open and she saw the woman's body being pulled out of the blackness directly overhead. Quickly she threw Ismailil to the left while she rolled to the right only seconds before the woman hit the ground with tremendous force right where they'd been lying.

No one moved.

The other prisoners, even with this tremendous distraction, had been too shocked to attempt to break free. Amri, who'd been in the void the shortest time, was lying silently, tears streaming down his face. Pandy rolled to Ismailil and gently nudged him. He flopped, unresponsive, to one side.

"Ismailil?" Pandy whispered. "Oh, come on . . . no. Ismailil? Oh, please . . ."

She pressed on his stomach lightly, she opened his mouth . . . she could think of nothing else to do.

"Oh, Ismailil, you've come so far. You guys are doing so well. Don't do this . . . don't do this. . . ." She began sobbing.

Finally the men, with the flat edges of their swords, began forcing everyone back into line.

"If we weren't paid by the head, I would have left them," Pandy heard one say to another.

"Anyone tries *anything* like that again, and we send the lot of you up there. Do you understand? One person gets a bright idea and you all die!" screamed the third man, moving his way to the head of the line.

The prisoners mumbled their acknowledgment.

Pandy was being herded back into formation.

The woman, lifeless, had been unshackled and rolled off the road. One man was preparing to do the same to Ismailil.

"No!" Pandy cried. "We can't just leave him!"

"Shut up!" His sword whacked her newly bruised shoulder.

"Please!" Pandy persisted.

"Do you want to drag him?" The man smirked.

"I will," she replied.

"Well, I won't."

Just as the man was about to release Ismailil, the boy gave a huge gasp, his little body arching in several spasms, arms and legs shaking.

"Thank you, Athena; thank you, Apollo! Thank you, Hades, for not taking him!" Pandy cried. "He's okay! See? He's okay! You can leave him chained up."

That, she thought, was probably the most ridiculous thing she had ever said.

Ismailil was brought back into the line, but Pandy moved forward to crawl directly alongside him, which forced Amri to her other side. Gently, uttering anything she could think of to keep the boys moving, she pushed, prodded, humored, and coaxed them—both in complete, wordless shock—forward with the rest of the prisoners.

She gave one last glance into the void, staring at the large gray sphere with the ring, already floating off somewhere else, and the two suspended lifeless bodies of the reddish men; eyes bulging, mouths agape, now and forever a part of the heavens.

CHAPTER FIFTEEN

Meanwhile...

"Prometheus?"

Artemis had materialized in the middle of the main room, her enormous silver-stringed bow scraping both the floor and ceiling at once. Taking a long look around, she sighed deeply. She'd been in Prometheus's house before, but she couldn't bring herself even to *try* to comprehend how someone could live in such cramped surroundings... *by choice!* She suddenly became thrilled she was a goddess with lovely, spacious apartments on Mount Olympus and the freedom to roam the world on a whim, if she chose.

"Prometheus?"

"Prometheus isn't here, Huntress," came a raspy voice from the stairwell. "Allow me to welcome you in his stead."

"What in Hades?" said Artemis.

"I am his houseguest, a simple wanderer," said the

figure emerging from the shadows. It was an old man in the ragged clothes of a beggar, leaning heavily on a walking stick, his hair almost white, his eyes bandaged, indicating blindness.

"What are you doing?" asked Artemis.

"I'm trying to find the food cupboards to pour you a proper glass of—"

"Prometheus? What are you *doing*?" she asked again, this time, a slight giggle to her voice.

The old man stopped in his tracks with a small sigh, then he stood upright and took off the blindfold.

"You knew it was me?"

"Um, how shall I put this delicately? *Yes!*" Artemis laughed out loud.

"Did I fool you for a second?" Prometheus asked.

"For a split second, maybe."

"Then maybe I can fool everyone for that long. Hey, what are you doing here? Where's Hermes?"

"Oh, when he got your prayer, he was just sitting down to his weekly father-son chat with Pan. Same thing every time: 'Pan, *son,* it's not nice to chase maidens and nymphs and then turn them into reeds or echoes or pine trees when they run away.' Hermes is getting tired of having to explain to their parents why these girls won't be coming home for evening meal. At any rate, he sent me to see if I could assist in some way . . . but he needs to see this getup for himself. Stay right there, don't move a muscle!"

With a silver flash she was gone. Ten seconds later, in another silver flash, Artemis and Hermes were both standing in the main room.

". . . no, Artie, the boy *doesn't* get it," Hermes was saying. "I'd like to spank him, but he's half goat, and that's some hard flesh down there."

He stopped and stared at Prometheus, then threw back his head with a laugh.

"Oh, Pro, pal, you have got to be kidding me! What, you've become an actor now? You're doing . . . lemme guess . . . *Oedipus II: The Reckoning*?"

"I need your help," Prometheus said quietly.

"By my winged helmet, what did you put in your *hair*?" Hermes was now doubled over, one arm clinging to Artemis.

"Fat and white ash. I need your help," Prometheus said again.

"This must be going around. First Hephaestus in that pirate beard and now you!"

"Hermes, I need you to help me."

Hermes straightened up, realizing that his dear friend wasn't even smiling.

"Uh, okay. Maybe yes, maybe no. Depends. But before you ask, you gotta tell me about the old man act."

"It's all part of it," Prometheus said. "I haven't heard from Pandy in over two weeks. The last thing she told me was that she was on her way to Jbel Toubkal."

"We know," Artemis said.

"Okay, okay, you know," Prometheus said, struggling to keep his voice calm. "I get it. You guys know everything. Where she's going and what's happening and I don't and that's fine. But I don't know how she *is*. The shells aren't working."

"It's the mountains, my friend," Hermes said. "Take it easy."

"I can't take it *easy*!" Prometheus cried. "Could you take it easy if something happened to Pan? Yes, he causes problems, but he's your *son*! Artie, could you take it easy if something happened to a baby animal that you loved? Huh? Could you?"

"No," Artemis replied.

"No way!" Prometheus said, his chest beginning to heave. "So here's what I need. You don't like this disguise, fine! Find me another. Anything you want. Just get me on top of that mountain without Zeus seeing. Because she's going to meet Atlas, and my brother will, quite probably, tear his only niece to pieces!"

"Pro . . . my friend . . . I want to help, but . . ."

"He will kill her, Hermes. And then where will we all be, huh? Where will the world be? He doesn't know who she is and we don't know what condition he's in!

When I last spoke to her, Pandora told me about a big black wall or something. I can't even guess what's going on. My point is, even with whatever power she's got, she's no match for him. I'm the only one he ever listened to growing up. I was his favorite brother. I'm the only one who can save her!"

"Prometheus," Artemis began.

"No! Listen . . . a disguise. Change me! Zeus won't know. And then you can just zap me there."

"Oh, yeah, zap you," Hermes said.

"You know, Hermes"—Artemis shifted slightly, clearing her throat—"with the right touches, we might be able to—"

"Oh, don't start with me, you!" Hermes cried. "Do you know what Dad would do?"

"But Prometheus does have one salient point: if Pandora is killed, then what becomes of the world?"

"Right! Right!" Prometheus stepped forward, shaking his index finger at Artemis. "What she said! Listen to her!"

"Do you know what you're asking? Both of you?" Hermes dropped his voice. "Pal, your kid is fine. She had a brief moment just now where we thought we were gonna lose her, but nothing happened; she just changed the constellation Gemini from triplets to twins . . . Who's gonna care, am I right?"

He gave a nervous little laugh, but Prometheus stared him down.

"Pro . . . I . . . I just can't," Hermes began.

Then Prometheus did something he'd never done before, to neither man nor god. Not when Zeus had captured him and chained him to the rock, not when he was brought before Zeus to receive the box, not even when he'd asked Sybilline to be his wife.

He got down on his knees.

"I'm begging you."

"Aw, sheesh, Pro." Hermes shuffled his feet.

"I'm begging you. My daughter will be killed and I'm the only one who can stop it. Nobody needs to know. I'll just be some old beggar who kept a Titan from slaughtering a little girl. Not even a smudge in the history scrolls."

There was a long, long silence as Hermes looked at the ceiling.

"Please?" Prometheus whispered.

Hermes looked at Artemis, who arched her eyebrows and smiled ever so slightly.

Then he looked down at Prometheus and began to speak.

CHAPTER SIXTEEN

Out and Up

When Pandy fell asleep the following night, she had noticed that the air around her, while still filthy and thick, was just slightly easier to breathe. But she was too exhausted to wonder why. Since their near-death experience the previous morning, she had worked feverishly to keep the boys in good spirits as they crawled forward, recounting the entire history of Greece (as much as she knew), telling about each of the gods, her beautiful white shepherd dog, and finally divulging almost all of her tale, except the really scary parts. After much humoring and prodding, she managed to get them to agree that they had both done something not terrifying, but *wonderful*, which no other human being would ever, ever do. They had actually *seen* the inside of the heavens. They had floated with the stars! Not even the gods did *that*. How special they were!

As the boys shifted their outlook from horrified to

enchanted, they each seemed to find new strength and crawled without so much as a whimper.

Now, as Pandy awoke two days after that experience, she saw that the black void was suspended farther off the ground . . . at least a full meter. And the farther the line crawled, the higher the bottom lifted and the easier it was to breathe. At last, the entire line of captives was able to stand. But there was no time to stretch; everyone was forced onward, marching on bruised knees and feet. They passed the captain of the guards, standing alongside the road.

"Excellent job!" he yelled to his men at the front and rear. "We didn't have to kill anybody and we lost only one. And it was just a woman. No matter."

No matter? This was not the first time that Pandy had listened to a man say a woman didn't matter: she flashed on the caliphs, the Channels of Earthly Displeasure, riding atop the slug tent at Wang Chun Lo's Caravan of Wonders, telling her they would not speak to her because she was female. What kind of a dummy would think that way? "Gods," she thought, staring at the captain's sandals as she trudged by, "would they treat their mothers that way?" She wondered what Athena or Artemis or Aphrodite or even Hera would say about that.

A yank on her shackles from Ismailil told her that she was moving too slowly. Lifting her eyes, she was suddenly confronted with a view of the tallest mountain she'd ever seen (except for Olympus) directly in front of her.

Jbel Toubkal.

She couldn't possibly guess how high it was.

Even through the dense air she could see the base of the mountain, covered with brush, rise into barren slopes that were covered with snow. But the highest peak, almost covered by the bottom of the heavens, was distinguished with a faint orange haze.

She realized they were now in a huge bell-shaped dome, surrounded on all sides by a circle of the black heavens. Pandy caught a faint whiff of smoke from an unseen source. The morning sun could barely penetrate into the dome, and everything was dull, almost color-less. Only the orange haze, reflecting off the snow on the mountaintops, was obvious.

Pandy tripped on a rock, nearly toppling herself as she stared up. Jbel Toubkal was holding up the canvas of the heavens at the highest point. Then the canvas spread out, like the top of Wang Chun Lo's tangerine tent, over the taller of the surrounding mountains, which held the heavens like tent poles.

An hour later, as the slaves arrived at the very base of the mountain, the line was stopped for only a few minutes as the captives were tossed a few pieces of flatbread and a water-skin was passed down the line. Pandy managed to sneak an apricot to Amri and a fig to

Ismailil while gulping down two slices of dried apple herself.

Then the line was moving again. Within the next five minutes, the road began to incline more steeply and narrowed to a slim, rocky path. Looking over her shoulder to check on Amri, Pandy saw another group of prisoners just emerging from underneath the void of the heavens many kilometers back.

For the rest of the day, they climbed. And climbed. Toward the evening, Pandy felt a sharp tug behind her and was convinced that Amri had somehow fallen off the path and was hanging off the side of the mountain.

But he had simply sat down, too tired to move any farther. Immediately, Pandy picked him up, determined to carry him to the top if necessary. It was then she realized that she herself was just not going to make it. She stumbled once and Amri clung to her neck. Then she stumbled again and just stayed on the road, every one of her muscles on fire, knowing she was about to be killed and tossed over the side. And not caring a bit as she fell asleep where she had fallen. She was done.

She snapped back into consciousness, not because Ismailil was shaking her, loudly crying that the rear guard was making his way up the hill, his sword drawn, but because there was something funny going on with her sandals.

All of a sudden, Pandy was jerked back upright. In

fact, it was only her sandals that straightened out; her legs (and the rest of her) just followed. On their own, her sandals began to move forward up the hill. Her leg muscles weren't being taxed at all. Yet she was "walking." She turned back to Amri; from the look on his face, he was experiencing the same phenomenon. Pandy gazed downward; his sandals were raised slightly off the ground, as were hers and Ismailil's. And then she noticed a small, bushy gray tail sticking out from under Ismailil's left heel. As she stifled a gasp, a small pinecone bounced sharply off her forehead. She looked around and finally spotted Dionysus's attack squirrel on a rock high above the path. She probably would have missed him if not for the fact that he was actually waving at her.

They were being carried on the backs of squirrels. Squirrels with the strength of Hercules.

The entire episode happened so fast that everyone was moving forward by the time the guard reached Amri.

"What happened?" he snarled.

"I just fainted . . . for a moment," Pandy said, trying to at least look like she was walking. "I'm sorry."

"Should have left you three in the darkness when we had the chance," the guard muttered as he tromped away. "Nothing but trouble."

As true darkness fell, the prisoners were herded off the path and onto a flat area halfway up the mountain.

The top of Jbel Toubkal was much closer, and the orange haze was now a glow. At this higher elevation, the cold descended quickly. The captain and his guards gathered underneath a small rocky overhang, built a fire, and roasted their evening meal, staying warm as they passed a wineskin.

The prisoners, exposed to freezing air, huddled together for warmth after eating their meager rations. Pandy gathered the boys underneath her mother's cloak, pulling it over all their heads, but it was still insufficient, and in minutes both Amri and Ismailil were shivering violently. She thought her furry wolfskin diary might help and was just undoing the pouch strap when she felt dozens of soft little paws crawling all over the top of the cloak.

"Uhhhh," Amri started up.

"No!" Pandy whispered. "Just wait."

The next instant, they felt a soft, warm weight completely covering the cloak. Pandy slowly poked her head out from underneath. In the light of the distant fire, she saw hundreds of small squirrels, curled into little balls, each one holding tight to another's tail, creating a thick fur blanket. And standing on top was the attack squirrel, blinking rather forcefully, as if telling her to go to sleep.

She managed a smile, snug and warm, and let herself drift off like the boys, who were already snoring softly.

The next morning, awakened by the thwack of a sword on her leg, Pandy flung off her cloak, which jolted the boys, and quickly got to her feet. The rest of the prisoners had already finished their morning scraps and were ready to march. Eating quickly and lining up, Pandy had no idea whether to expect the squirrels' help or not. But as the line moved back onto the path and her feet were solidly hitting the ground, she knew it had been a one-time-only occurrence. She looked at the boys. Their strides seemed strong and confident.

"Thank you, Dionysus," she said softly.

Slowly, the line made its way steadily up the mountain. In the early afternoon, they hit the first scattered patches of snow, and Pandy covered Amri with her cloak as best she could. The air was much thinner now; everyone was breathing in great heaving gulps. Soon there was nothing but a steep drop to one side and a solid wall of ice and snow to the other.

As night fell again, the path began to wind around the far, dark side of the mountain, snaking its way back and forth. The warm orange glow was not only lighting the path but also causing the snow to melt, making the last fifty meters slushy and desperately cold. With the bottom of the heavens once again fairly close above their heads, the line of freezing prisoners crested the final ridge and gazed down into what appeared to be a village or city of some sort nestled in a shallow crater on top of the mountain. The orange glow came from many fires burning bright, illuminating various structures and people bustling about.

At first glance, Pandy thought the village was rather ordinary. But the longer she looked, the faster she realized that there was nothing ordinary about it.

CHAPTER SEVENTEEN
On Top

The narrow path that had sloped upward for the past two days now descended, gently but quickly, along the inside rim of the mountaintop crater. The line was heading down.

All except one person.

"Go, Pandy! Go," Amri pleaded.

The rear guard was almost upon them and Amri was pushing on her arm while Ismailil was yanking the chain that held them together. But Pandy was nearly paralyzed.

There was so much activity Pandy didn't know what to focus on first. She saw women and children rushing about, dragging heavy sacks of . . . something, or packing what looked like mud into circular shapes, or carrying huge jars of water. Other women were huddled around strange glowing domes. There were old men tending fires. There was smoke everywhere. She noticed dozens of guards and hundreds of reddish creatures posted around the entire circumference of the top ridge— as much as she could see of it in the darkness and smoke. Then she saw two enormous huts built on low platforms. Outside of one hut, a long line of prisoners waited to enter through a cloth-covered opening.

These sights made some sense to Pandy, as she was now being shoved down along the path.

What she could not comprehend, what she had willed herself to mentally ignore . . .

. . . were the columns.

Hundreds and hundreds of them everywhere—thick and brown, rising up at least twenty meters into the air, well above the highest point on the surrounding ridge.

And on top of each column was a man.

"No," Pandy thought. "No, that isn't quite right."

It was, to be precise, half a man.

Only the upper torso of each was visible, sticking out of the top, arms raised high, back muscles straining. Some of the men were yelling in short bursts at the top of their lungs, others were silent and red faced. Still others were hunched over, their arms hanging limply at their sides, backs crunched and misshapen. But all of them together were really doing only one thing.

Each of these men was holding up the heavens.

Pandy suddenly thought she might be quite sick.

She tried to turn away, but her curiosity got the better

of her. She and the boys had been sucked through the bottom of the heavens and into the void—why weren't these men being sucked through as well? There *was* an answer, and she knew she'd find it . . . eventually.

Her group moved into the village. Pandy saw there were more columns under construction; column sections were strewn all over as groups of boys and girls, attached to ropes and pulleys, lifted ridiculously heavy column pieces onto one another. Snaking their way through the commotion, the captives passed by huge mixing pits where women stirred mud with long wooden poles while others skirted wide wells that went straight into the heart of the mountain. They crisscrossed paths with men, weeping or begging or cursing, being led in chains. They passed the strange domes, which, Pandy now saw, were actually crude ovens, slowly baking column sections over low fires. And they passed by columns everywhere. Pandy forced herself not to look up.

As their group joined the end of the long line of other prisoners, they stopped just to the side of one of the two low platforms. Although the building on it was obviously very makeshift, stones and mortar hastily slapped together, the smell gave its purpose away. This building housed the food cupboards, drainage boards, and cooking area for the village.

"Lemon rinds!" a young female voice yelled in Greek, and Pandy's heart flipped over.

"Gods!" she muttered softly. Alcie? Was Alcie alive, here, just a single stone wall away?

She was about to call out when the speaker, a brown-skinned girl, perhaps twenty years old, left the preparation hut and hurried to a nearby well.

"He wants lemon rinds in his water!" she called back over her shoulder. "Find them!" She saw Pandy gaping at her.

"What are you looking at?" the girl asked.

Pandy quickly looked down as the girl went on her way.

No, not Alcie . . . of course not. Pandy cursed her own stupidity: they were dead, all of them . . . her two best friends, her beloved dog, and the youth who was only meant to be their guard on a short voyage. Apollo's chariot had crashed, she was certain. How lame to think she would ever see them again.

As she began to sob, biting hard on her lip to keep the boys from seeing, the line moved forward a few meters, and another group was herded into the hut on the second platform and whatever lay beyond the cloth-covered door.

The sunlight had vanished hours before: it was easily after the middle of the night. There was no letup, how-ever, in the noise and pace of the work around them. While some workers slept in clusters on the open ground, others took their place until yet another shift change. There was never a quiet moment, Pandy saw.

None of the captives were allowed to sit down; everyone stood in place until the line moved again. The scent wafting from the food preparation hut, while not the most appetizing thing Pandy had smelled, still reminded them all how hungry they were. Soon two gray-haired women emerged from the food hut, one carrying a large wooden tray from which she tossed the prisoners scraps of meat, the other passing a water-skin down the line. Biting into her meat, Pandy realized it was mainly gristle, fat, and joint. She secretly spit it out and motioned to Amri and Ismailil to do the same (although Ismailil refused until he almost cracked a tooth on a piece of bone). Then she slyly snuck the boys handfuls of dried fruit.

Slowly the line inched forward.

An hour later, they were within three meters of the covered door and Pandy was trying to see if she could sleep standing up.

"Morpheus?" she called inside her mind. "Morpheus . . . are you there?"

"No," came the reply.

"Oh, good. Hi. Can I just have a little dream?"

"Stop it."

"What?"

"Stop asking. I'm not coming. Hermes told me not to help you right now," Morpheus answered.

"Why not?"

"Because you're not supposed to be sleeping now, Pandora. You've got to be alert."

"Just a nap?"

"No."

"A tiny one? I'm so tired. Pleeeeeeeeeeeeeeeeease!"

"No. Can't hear you. Not listening. Lalalalalalalalala," Morpheus began to sing.

Ismailil, who'd been slapping himself on his arms to keep from sleeping, gave Pandy a swat. Her eyes flew wide open.

"Please stay awake!" he whispered.

"Good boy!" said Morpheus, his laughter fading in Pandy's mind.

"I'm awake. I'm awake," she said.

Amri, however, had finally given up and was out cold, propped against Pandy's hip. Throwing her arm about his little shoulder, she slumped back and found herself leaning against two huge, pinkish, fuzzy logs stacked on top of each other. She had no idea what they were and didn't much care; all she felt was soft. Even the strands of thin black fuzz protruding from all over the log, like black strings, were kinda soft.

It was the most comfortable *anything* she'd felt in weeks. She nestled in and was just letting her eyelids sag again as her fingers wound in and out of the black strings. Without thinking, she tugged on one, noticing how the substance around it moved outward as she pulled. Suddenly, she tugged the black string right out of the log.

Immediately, the log jerked back and a small red blotch appeared where the string had been.

With a muffled shriek, Pandy sprang away, still holding the string but now staring at it . . . realizing that it was a big hair and she'd been leaning against a ginormous pair of legs.

The incredibly oversized legs (and the wide hem of a man's toga) were sticking horizontally out of an opening in the hut. She'd missed seeing it at first because this larger opening was hidden by some broken and discarded sections of column. Suddenly the legs (whoever they belonged to had obviously been reclining) were drawn up and into the opening and then Pandy saw a seated figure many meters tall—too tall to really see the face, but she could easily make out the bottom of a long, swishy black beard.

She was thrown off balance as Amri was roughly shoved forward. Another group of prisoners had joined the end of the line. This time, however, there was an immediate commotion back in the food hut.

"Just let me finish this . . . soup, stew . . . whatever it is!" A woman's voice rose above the din.

"It's your turn," called another, angrier than the first. "Water the line!"

In the distance, the side door to the hut flew open, and two women emerged: a redheaded woman with a plate of meat and a woman with a water-skin, black hair falling around her face. Beginning at the new end of the line, the woman with the meat took only minutes to reach the man now standing behind Amri. The water-skin was passed more slowly. The dark-haired woman wasn't looking at anyone, and her impatience was clear.

"Excuse me," Pandy called as the man behind Amri finished a giant swig. "Could these boys get just a little more water?"

The woman, her back to Pandy, jutted her hip out as she slouched on one leg and shook her head.

"If I give it to them," she said, turning to look Pandy in the eye, "then I have to give . . . oh . . . oh! Ahhhh! Amri!"

Dropping the skin, she took a giant step and scooped the little boy up in her arms.

Amri, who had been sleeping peacefully against Pandy, woke up and, at first, feeling a fresh set of arms upon him, struggled with his new captor. Then he looked the woman in the face.

"Mother!"

"Mother!" yelled Ismailil.

"My sons!" she cried, rushing to Ismailil, the three of

them holding on to one another in a tight huddle, which naturally included Pandy. There was so much clamor that several of the women in the food hut gathered at the door, and prisoners in line, strangers to each other, strained for a glimpse of the commotion. Suddenly, people who didn't know the person next to them were clasping hands and smiling to one another.

After many tears and many kisses, the boys introduced Pandy.

"She saved us, Mother!" Ismailil said.

"She saved my leg!" cried Amri. "She thinks she's a snake. And she can talk to squirrels!"

Looking at the food hut, Pandy saw that the redheaded woman was moving back toward the boys' mother. Suddenly, one of the gray-haired women called out of the doorway.

"Let her be!"

"She's slacking!" the redhead spat.

"I said, let her *be*! She's found her children. That's cause enough to rejoice."

The boys' mother stood to face Pandy.

"I'm Ghida," she said. Then she paused, shaking slightly. "I . . . I don't know what to say."

"It's okay. You don't have to say anything. We had fun, right guys?"

"We were in the heavens!" Ismailil said.

"We touched the stars." Amri nodded.

"What?" Ghida cried.

"Uh, there was, like, an accident," Pandy said quickly. "A woman tried to escape, but believe me, your boys are fine."

"We did something that even her gods never do!" said Amri.

"Knowing you two," Ghida said, tenderly touching Amri's face, "I don't doubt it."

The next instant, Pandy and the boys were yanked forward.

"Oh, no," Ghida said. "You're going in."

"Mother!" shouted the boys at once.

"It's all right." Ghida kept pace with the line as it moved toward the second hut. "There's nothing to be afraid of. And I will find you . . . both of you. All right? Amri, look at me! I will come to you!"

Ghida stopped short as a guard brandished his sword in her face.

"Move back!"

"Don't worry," Pandy called, just as Ismailil disappeared behind the cloth curtain. "I'll take care of them."

Suddenly, Ghida was gone from view and Pandy's head was forced to her chest.

"Keep it that way!" someone commanded.

Eyes down, the entire line was herded into rows facing one end of the hut. Off to one side, Pandy caught sight of a group of guards, just waiting. After the captives had settled, no one so much as flinched for a long time.

After several minutes of silence, they suddenly noticed a new sound: a light snoring was coming from the warm end of the room. There was a muffled conversation between two head guards.

"Just wake him," said one finally.

There was a sound of footsteps, someone saying, "Sir, the new line is ready," and then an enormous volley of harrumphing and sputtering.

"Oh, and I was having the nicest dream—something about clouds, and there was a duck, and then my mother was there, only she wasn't my mother but a green skink."

"Sir, the prisoners?" the guard reiterated.

"Ah, yes. Oh, goody . . . newbies! Yeah!"

"Eyes up, all of you," said the guard.

Pandy looked up with everyone else, into the enormous, sleepy-eyed face of her uncle Atlas, Bearer of the Heavens.

CHAPTER EIGHTEEN

Just a Trim

He had to be, Pandy thought, at least fifteen times the size of a normal man, maybe twenty. Gods, she realized, Atlas was larger than Zeus! His arms were like tree trunks and his chest was shaped like a wine vat. His muscles had muscles. He could only sit or recline; standing would have torn the roof off the building. His skin was whitish pink from having the dark heavens so close to him for eternity and never really seeing the sun. His teeth, she saw when he yawned, were rounded and bulbous, like large onions. But it was his hair that caused Pandy's skin to prickle. It was everywhere. The thick black hairs on his legs were only the start. The hair on his head stuck out at least half a meter on all sides; his eyebrows were one black snake across his forehead. His arms were covered with thick patches of hair protruding at odd angles, and his black beard, braided and beaded in some places, which Pandy had only glimpsed outside, hung down almost a full meter. Then Pandy saw his tusk.

Tusk?

She waited for him to move his head, even a little. When he did, to yawn yet again, she saw that it wasn't a tusk at all but a giant yellowish gray hair, twice as thick as any other, about as big around as a big squash and at least a meter in length, growing straight out of one nostril.

"Very well, newbies," Atlas said. "Where, oh where, shall I put you all, hmmm?"

One by one, he assigned tasks.

"You: fire pit number 8 . . . you, nice arms: bearer . . . bearer . . . bearer, northern mountain . . . feeder, eastern mountain . . ."

Pandy realized the surrounding mountains also had slaves in columns on their tops. Atlas probably intended to cover the mountains of the known world with millions of columns, all to do his job.

". . . bearer . . . water-well number 37 . . . feeder . . . feeder, northern mountain . . . you, can you climb a ladder? Good: used-man retrieval . . . um, oven number 5 . . . you, good arms, but you're a kid: pulleys . . . for you: main mixing pit . . . bearer . . . bearer, southern mountain . . . you: perimeter sentry . . ."

Then, about halfway through the line, Atlas just closed his eyes and dozed. When the head guards woke him gently several moments later, he harrumphed and gazed around as if he didn't know exactly where he was. He stretched, yawning, and ran his giant hands through his hair.

"Oh, my. I need another haircut," he said to no one in particular.

"Barbers!" called a guard. The call was echoed outside.

"Would you like to continue?" the guard asked Atlas.

"After my haircut."

"Yes, sir."

The rest of the line waited as two young Persian barbers entered the hut through an opening at the back, followed by a single assistant, a girl, carrying a large cloth sack. Quickly, the assistant opened the sack and handed one barber a pair of heavy shears. The other barber stamped his foot and clomped back to the opening.

"Hurry it up!" Pandy heard him yell.

"I'm sorry," came a small voice, growing nearer. "I'm sorry."

And there, suddenly, barely managing two big ladders and a long broom, was Iole.

"Ahhh." Pandy choked loudly and gripped the boys so hard that they both cried out. As those closest to her turned to look, she quickly put her head down.

Her mind reeled. She was shocked—stunned, certainly, but she realized that she was happier at that moment than she'd ever been before in her life. Nothing was wrong, everything was right. Iole was alive. And if Iole was alive, then Alcie had to be . . . she just had to be.

"What's going on back there?" yelled one head guard.

Another guard, in the group, smacked Pandy with the flat side of his sword.

"What?" he barked.

"I'm sorry," Pandy said loudly, looking up and craning her head high. "Leg cramp. It was me. My bad."

Then she locked eyes with Iole, who dropped the ladders on one barber's foot.

"Sorry! Sorry," Iole said, trying to get a good hold on them again.

"Shut it," said the first guard to Pandy.

"You bet," Pandy replied, settling back.

"Let's make this a full body trim," Atlas was saying to the barbers. "I'm feeling all-over fuzzy."

Iole and the other girl positioned the ladders against Atlas. As one barber unbraided and debeaded the long beard, the other went to work trimming the leg hairs. Pandy pretended to simply look around, her eyes always coming back to Iole. Iole tried to look like she was concentrating, but she was shaking badly and she kept handing the wrong implements to her barber.

"I said 'straight razor'!" he cried.

"Sorry," she sputtered, handing him the right tool, her gaze drifting out to Pandy.

From the legs to the arms to the massive barrel chest, climbing up and down the ladder, the barber razored each and every black hair. Iole would step forward every few seconds to sweep away the cut hairs with the broom.

"You're giving me nice points, right?" Atlas asked the barber, semidozing. "You're not making them blunt?"

"Beautiful points, sir, absolutely."

"And you," Atlas said to the other, "when you're done trimming, I want ruby and ivory beads this time."

"Excellent choice, sir," said the barber, slowly scissoring each beard hair individually.

After twenty minutes, Pandy locked eyes with Iole for the hundredth time and finally got up the courage to mouth the word "Alcie."

Iole gave an almost imperceptible nod of her head.

Pandy pursed her lips in a tight smile, then she mouthed the word "Homer."

Iole nodded again, but her brow furrowed deeply.

Something was wrong with Homer.

As Pandy watched, Iole leaned the broom against the far wall and casually raised both arms above her head and turned her palms up, squatting for a split second. Then she lowered her arms as if it had only been a momentary stretch.

But Pandy understood.

Somewhere on the mountain, buried to his waist in a column, Homer was a bearer.

"Are we boring you, Iole?" asked her barber.

"No, sir," she said. "I'm sorry."

"Problem?" asked Atlas.

"Oh . . . no, sir," said the barber. "It's just my assistant. If it would please you, I could use another."

"Fine," Atlas said, then promptly dozed off again.

The two barbers, moving at lightning speed, were almost done cutting and shaping the huge mane on Atlas's head. Then they stopped abruptly. One of the guards woke Atlas.

"Sir," one barber said, stepping forward, "we are about to begin your face."

Suddenly, Atlas sat bolt upright, which startled everyone in the room. Pandy immediately looked at Iole, who met her gaze with an expression that Pandy read as "pay attention."

Working first on the ears, then the heavy brow, then the cheeks, the two men slowly moved inward toward the nose. Pausing for a second to breathe deeply, one barber used both hands to grab the thick, yellow gray hair and lightly move it out of the way as his partner set about snipping the other nostril hairs.

"Would you like points, sir?" he asked.

"Just do it!" Atlas growled.

Pandy had all but forgotten about the strange hair, so different from all the others. In fact, if she completely ignored the fact that he was gargantuan, it was the only odd thing about her uncle. Now she watched Atlas clenching his hands tightly, his knuckles snow white, his teeth set, breath issuing forth in short spurts.

"Don't nick it!" he hissed.

"Nowhere near it, sir," the barber replied, but he had to stop every so often and un-tense his hands.

Why wouldn't her uncle want that horrible hair gone?

Atlas couldn't be in pain, she thought. Then it dawned on her—he was nervous.

She looked at Iole, who cocked her head slightly. Suddenly, she understood.

"Oh," she said softly.

"What?" whispered Amri.

"Nothing," Pandy whispered back.

All at once, the barbers backed away from Atlas's face like it was white hot and scuttled down their ladders. Now, with all the rest of his hair shorn, the giant yellow gray nose hair was even more prominent.

"All done, sir," one barber said.

"Ah, the Persians." Atlas laughed, once again completely relaxed and slightly jovial. "No one cuts hair like the Persians. Now where were we?"

And, as the barbers began to collect their tools, dumping them into the bag Iole held open, Atlas continued with his assignment delegation.

"You: oven number 18 . . . you, can you cook?

Excellent: kitchen . . . bearer . . . feeder, western mountain . . . bearer . . ."

Next was Ismailil.

"Wow, you're puny: mixing pit number two."

Suddenly, Ismailil was unchained and about to be pulled away. Frantic, Amri called out to his brother.

"What gives?" said Atlas.

"They're brothers," Pandy spoke up. "Sir, if it would please you, they are brothers."

"Aw, that's cute," Atlas said, looking at Amri. "And you're even punier! Puny is cute. Okay, put 'em together."

As Amri was unchained he looked up at Pandy.

"But, Pan—!"

"No!" She silenced him, not wanting her name to be revealed. "This is good. You just go."

She bent down.

"Go," she whispered to the little boys she now considered to be like her own brothers. "I'll find you. Just go and do what they say."

She quickly kissed each boy on top of his head and they were led away.

Then she was alone.

"You," Atlas began, and Iole dropped the bag, spilling all the shears and razors.

"Oh." She looked up, innocent, trying to make her eyes impossibly large. "I am so terribly sorry."

"I *do* need a new assistant," said her master.

"I *could* use some help," Iole agreed, looking directly at Atlas.

"Bold girl!" the barber cried. "I meant to get rid of—"

"Fine," Atlas interrupted, glancing at Pandy. "You . . . with her."

Pandy was unchained and shoved to the end of the room. Iole's barber barely glanced at her.

"Clean up and bring her to the tent," he muttered to Iole as the two men exited, backward, with the other assistant.

"Um," Iole said to Pandy, grabbing one ladder, "could you get the other one?"

"Sure," Pandy said.

Pandy was moving toward the opening at the rear when Iole caught her by the arm and secretly gave Pandy a tight squeeze.

"You have to back out," she said.

"Oh, okay." Pandy stifled an unexpected sob. The two ladders kept colliding and getting stuck in each other as the girls left the large room.

Pandy was very busy trying to decide which piece of information was greater: the knowledge that her best friends were alive and right there, or the fact that Laziness was hiding in her uncle's big, ugly nose hair.

CHAPTER NINETEEN

Old Men

"She's here!" Prometheus all but screamed. He tried to straighten up, but in disguising them both as old men, Hermes had given Prometheus such a hunch to his back that, as he practically danced with excitement and joy, he looked like a deranged crab.

"And you'd like *everyone* to know?" Hermes replied, also hunched over, but not as badly.

"She's here!" Prometheus whispered, shaking his withered, gnarled hands up and down.

"That's good." Hermes concentrated on his wooden pole. "Let everyone see how excited you are about something in this gods-forsaken place. *Ixnay on the aking-shay*. Start stirring."

"I'm just so . . . so . . ."

"Cheese it, the rat!" Hermes spat.

A guard was swiftly approaching from across the compound, knocking slaves out of his path. He strode directly up to Prometheus, almost knocking him into the mud pit.

"Where've you been, old man? I sent you for my morning meal an hour ago. Your knobby knees so bent you can't walk faster than this?"

Prometheus realized he had forgotten his task and looked imploringly at Hermes . . . who just rolled his eyes behind the guard and flicked at his nose as if he were flicking a fly. Immediately, in the sack hanging across one shoulder, Prometheus felt the weight of two apples and a wedge of goat's-milk cheese.

"And it had better still be hot, you wretch," spat the guard, now bearing down on Prometheus, "or you'll be mixing this mud from the bottom up."

In a flash, Prometheus felt the apples and cheese transform into a clay jar full of creamed oats.

"Here you are, sir." Prometheus handed the jar to the guard and smiled an absolutely toothless smile. "Nice and hot."

"Get back to work."

As the guard walked back across the compound and settled himself with his comrades, Hermes flicked his finger again.

"What did you just do?" asked Prometheus.

"Not a thing," Hermes said. "I shall deny any part in turning a pot full of oats into a stomach full of worms."

"Okay. Did you hear what I said? She's—"

"I have never seen so much dirt in my life," Hermes said, before Prometheus could say another word. "I have never been so dirty. I have never tasted so much dirt. I have dirt in my eyes, my nose, my ears, my teeth—"

"You still *have* teeth."

"—I am a *god*, thank you very much, I get *some* benefits—my hair, my armpits, under my fingernails, and between my toes. Ah, the joys of friendship. All right, she's here. Now, what are you going to do?"

Prometheus sighed.

"Nothing."

"Thaaaat's right. That's the deal. Look but don't hug. She never knows you're *you*, even if you have to help her. That way if Zeus ever finds out and asks her, she'll be able to answer honestly. So, where did you see her?"

"Oh, Hermes." Prometheus stopped stirring. He stared into the dawn cutting through the surrounding blackness, illuminating the hectic village. "She was dragging a ladder out of Atlas's quarters. She was with her friend Iole and from the way they were crying and pinching each other, she must have just arrived. Oh, it was so good to see her! And . . . and . . . she had this air about her, Hermes. She's changed. It's like . . . my little girl left home and now there's this capable, strong, almost . . . mature . . . young woman in her place. You know, I think if I had known what she'd become, what she's becoming, I might not have pressed so hard to be here. I think she can handle—"

"Great! We can go!"

"No," Prometheus said calmly, not missing a beat, "*almost* anything. Almost. Except my brother. He had another haircut, by the looks of things. I think Pandora's been assigned to the barbers. I bumped into them right before I saw her and they were talking about training the new girl and Atlas's wild nose hair."

"And I thought Demeter's hair was wacky," Hermes said.

"My friend, this is the first time in months that I feel anything at all except despair. And you know what that feeling is?"

"Lay it on me," Hermes said.

"I'm starving."

"Good sign, I'm happy! Check in your cloth sack."

Prometheus felt around and, out of view of the other slaves, pulled out a perfectly roasted piece of lamb.

"Wonderful!" He smiled. "And for those of us who have to gum our food?"

"Fine. Put it back." Hermes sighed.

In the sack, Prometheus felt the lamb change in his hand to three pitted, overripe apricots.

"Thank you."

"Pleasure," Hermes answered.

Gumming the apricots, Prometheus ambled over to

two young boys, newly arrived that morning, who were struggling with one mixing stick between them.

"Hello . . . let me help you," he said before he realized that they spoke not a word of Greek.

He patted his chest and introduced himself.

"I'm Theus . . . Theus."

The larger of the two understood.

"Ismailil," he said, hitting his own chest, then pointing to the other, smaller boy, "Amri."

CHAPTER TWENTY

Together Again

Iole kept Pandy silent as the two girls stowed the ladders against the side of a small hut. Then she led Pandy back around several columns and into the main room of the barbers' lodgings; it was crude, but unlike most of the other structures, it had a roof. Iole bowed, as did Pandy, to the two Persian men, now tending a bronze teapot hanging over a little fire, and ushered Pandy through a privacy curtain and into a small side storeroom. Pandy was about to throw her arms around Iole when Iole motioned to the other assistant, already asleep in a corner. The two girls crept into the opposite corner to sit on a dirty carpet and hugged each other tightly, weeping into their cloaks.

"When we saw you fall," Iole sputtered, "we thought you were dead. But then, as the days passed, I was convinced, Pandy—I was *convicted*—that you were still alive. Alcie, too. We just knew it in our hearts. We knew we would *feel* differently if you were gone."

"Me too," Pandy whispered. "I had the feeling that somehow you guys were okay. I just don't think the gods would have let us come this far only to kill us now. Where's Alcie?"

"She's a feeder. But her shift is over at dawn. She should be here any minute."

"What's a feeder?" asked Pandy.

"They're the ones who bring water and food, if you can call it that, up to the men bearing the heavens. *That's* what they're doing, you know. *They're* doing it, Pandy!"

"I know."

Then Iole's voice began to tremble.

"Homer's up there, Pandy."

"So I guessed. But we'll get him down. Okay, tell me everything you know. Where were you, how did you get here, and are you certain Laziness is in my uncle's nose?"

"Oh, Gods." Iole sighed. "How do I even commence?"

Iole began the tale of their incredible voyage: Apollo landing the chariot, their kidnap by Atlas's pirates, the *Syracusa*, catching and imprisoning Misery . . .

"What?" Pandy cried. The girl in the opposite corner raised her head and glared at Pandy and Iole.

"What?" Pandy whispered.

"We have it," Iole said, grinning. Quietly, she stood up and pulled her pouch down from a rickety shelf. She withdrew the small wooden box surrounded by the square adamant shackles and gingerly handed it to Pandy.

"Oh, you would have been so proud of Alcie," Iole went on. "She was fierce, like an Amazon. She didn't really have a plan, but she was determined. She just kept saying 'We'll figure it out!' And then, once we had Misery in the box, she remembered that we'd been chained with adamant shackles, so we snuck to the armory and met Hephaestus."

"You're kidding," Pandy said, taking the box.

"I'm not. And he created these," Iole went on, pointing to the bands around the box. "And that's when we knew. We knew at that point at least you were still alive. Why would anyone help us, without you there, if they didn't think we'd all meet up again?"

"Brilliant, as usual. We'll figure out how to transfer Misery into the main box later."

At that moment, a heavy cloth covering an opening at the other end of the little room was thrust aside and a hooded figure stood in the dim morning light.

"Iole, he doesn't look good. His skin is turning pink."

Alcie threw back her hood and was just about to enter when she saw Pandy.

In an instant, Pandy was on her feet . . . but Alcie just stared, until her lower lip started to quiver and her eyes filled with tears, blinding her. She clutched at the heavy cloth. When Pandy realized that Alcie couldn't move, she crossed the room and embraced her other best friend.

Pandy led Alcie back to the corner, where the other two waited several minutes for Alcie to stop crying and heaving enough to be able to speak.

"Tangerines," she joked quietly, gripping Pandy's hand, "this is such a groovy way to start the day."

Pandy and Iole grinned.

"Okay," Iole said, "I was just finishing the part where we captured Misery."

"Neat, huh?" said Alcie, hiccupping a bit from all the crying.

"So cool," agreed Pandy.

"You know, Homer wasn't even around; it was just Iole and me. But Homer wrote some amazing stuff during the whole thing. He's related to the *other* Homer, the famous one. Oh, Gods, Pandy, do you know what's happened to Homer? Lemons! He's been up on a column for three days."

"We'll get him down," Pandy said. "But first I have so many questions."

"Me too," said Alcie.

"Okay, did you guys crawl under the heavens?" Pandy asked.

"Of course, it's the only way in," Iole said.

"Did you lose anyone?" Pandy asked.

"Lose anyone?" Alcie asked.

"Did anyone get sucked up inside?"

"I saw a bird get trapped, but a person?"

"Moldy apples! No!"

Pandy recounted the poor woman's attempted escape from her line and Pandy's subsequent moments in the black void.

"Chewed-up olive pits!"

"Listen, before I ask anything else . . ." Pandy turned to Iole. "Do you have any idea why things were able to be sucked into the void down below and why the men are able to hold it up here?"

"She does," Alcie said.

"I do," said Iole.

"She told me the first morning when I snuck in here for some shut-eye. I couldn't sleep, thinking about Homer. So she told me her theory. I went out like a candle flame."

"I hypothesize that it's because the bottom of the heavens is constructed like a netting or webbing of some kind," Iole began. "Up here, it's tight as a festival drum, like it's supposed to be. But down below, it's completely stretched out, the way a fisherman's net stretches when it's full of fish and you can poke your hand through. Close to the earth, the netting is being stretched wide and that's why things can get sucked up inside."

"Yawn. Okay, prunes. Start back at the beginning and

then we have to talk about Homer. What happened when you fell?" Alcie cried.

Pandy told them everything: Dionysus, the pine-nut-cup ride down the mountain, Ismailil and Amri, hiding and being caught, the squirrels, and the journey up Jbel Toubkal.

"How'd you get assigned here?" Alcie asked Pandy.

"Because I am incredibly clever," Iole cut in.

"Now, about Homer," Alcie began.

"Wait, if you're a feeder, aren't you in another group? How do you get to come here every morning?" Pandy asked.

"Puh-leeze!" Alcie said. "I'm supposed to be sleeping, and no one guards a group of passed-out prisoners. I just sneak away. There's no way any of us are getting off this mountain, and as long as I report tonight, no one cares."

"Plus, all I would have to do is say she's with me and anyone would back off," Iole said.

"Oh, and don't think she doesn't just love that!" Alcie said, under her breath.

"What do you mean?" Pandy asked.

"The barbers are treated like Greek philosophers . . . or even actors! Complete respect. They get meat and wine, a hut with a roof. Unrestricted movement about the compound, and since I'm an assistant—"

"Constantly reminding me." Alcie sighed.

"—I can come and go pretty much as I please with this."

Iole tapped a tiny, very dull pair of metal shears hanging around her neck on the same chain as the Eye of Horus.

"But why?" Pandy asked again.

"It's all about the hair," Alcie said.

"Atlas's hair grows so fast that he needs it cut every day."

"That's freaky. He's Dad's brother," Pandy said. "Dad's hair doesn't grow that fast."

"It has to be part of his enchantment," Iole said.

"You saw *the hair,* right?" Alcie asked.

Before Pandy could respond, Iole went on.

"Apparently, he had become quite hirsute—"

"Hairy," Alcie interrupted.

"Thank you," Pandy said.

"—when he set down the heavens, so when he started recruiting Roman soldiers in the area to be his hench-men, the first thing he demanded was barbers. He loves to just sit and be snipped."

"But you saw *the hair,* right?" Alcie repeated, drop-ping her voice.

"Of course," said Pandy.

"It's Laziness," said Iole.

"I think so too. It has to be," said Pandy. "Laziness is something that would have to be on or in my uncle to make him forget his responsibility and set down the heavens. It's the only obvious . . . what's the word?"

"Transmogrified? Metamorphosed? Mutated?" Iole said.

". . . mutated thing about him. He froze up when the barbers got too close to that nose hair."

"It's never been cut," Iole said. "It's been nicked twice over the past weeks and both times he's flown into a rage. It's the most action anyone's seen out of him. He picked up his barbers and threw them both off the mountain. The current barbers are replacements for the replacements. But I hear them talking, and they say the longer the hair gets, the lazier he becomes. It's like a constant dose of lotus leaves."

"Well, even if it were to be cut, it would simply grow back. It has to be torn out at the root. Maybe when he's sleeping," Pandy mused.

"Good luck getting around the guards," Alcie said.

"We're pretty good at creating diversions," Pandy reminded her. "At any rate, we have to get it in the box as fast as possible."

"But, Pandy, we're gonna get Homer down, right?" Alcie said, the worry growing in her voice.

"Duh! As soon as we get Laziness . . ."

"NO!" Alcie yelled, and the girl in the corner shifted in her sleep. "Now! Figs. I know this is *your* quest and *you* make the decisions, okay? And . . . and we didn't even know how to do it before you got here, but now, with your powers, we can think of something to get him down first!"

"Alcie, keep your voice down," Iole cautioned.

Alcie went right on in a quieter tone.

"Pandy, he's big and strong and the only time I feel super safe, really, is when he's around! And he's *so* cute . . . and he's the first one in a long time who likes me. A lot. Me! Oh, pears! And he's smart. And he thinks I'm . . . And he's, like, gorgeous, and that's gonna be wrecked if you . . . we . . ."

Pandy looked at Iole.

"Long story. Tell you later."

"Alcie," Pandy replied, turning back to her friend, "calm down, okay? As soon as Laziness goes into the box, my uncle will remember his vow and his responsibility and take up the heavens again. I'm sure of it. Then the burden will be lifted off of everyone, including the men on those other mountains."

Alcie went white.

"What? Alcie, what?" Pandy cried.

"Iole, prunes . . . prunes, Iole. Tell her. I don't even know how to say it," Alcie whimpered.

"Pandy, we've determined from everything we've seen and heard that each man lasts only four days on a column. That's how long it takes for the weight of the heavens to, basically, to crush the bones. It doesn't kill them, but it compresses them, and, even though the sun is far away, it still hardens the skin and turns it red and—"

"And turns normal, full-grown men into those tiny, shriveled, reddish creatures," Pandy finished, grasping the full horror. It would take only a year, maybe less, for Atlas to use up every last man on earth. And then what would happen?

"Right," Iole said. "We arrived here three days ago at dawn. Homer was baked into a column almost immediately. Today is his fourth day. That means that even though Homer is stronger than almost anybody we know and he might last a little longer, he really only has until tonight."

"And then he's a 'used-man,'" Alcie whispered. "I'll love him even if he's shriveled, by Athena's teeth, I will! But I'll have to pick him up and carry him everywhere. I'll be toting my little red boyfriend under my arm wherever I go!"

"That's what you meant when you came in saying that his skin was turning pink," Pandy said to Alcie.

Alcie nodded.

"And he'll never be the same. At least we don't think so. Gods, that much weight on a body? The effects must be irreversible," Iole said. "Look, I know Alcie's reasoning sounds a little self-centered right now . . ."

"Hey!"

"It does. But you have to admit, Pandy," Iole went on,

"Homer's been invaluable on the quest. And now that you're here, we have to try."

"Oh, Gods, Pandy . . . apples, apples, apples!" Alcie said, the panic creeping back into her voice. "If we don't do something, we'll lose him. *I'll* lose him. The only guy I will ever love will be half a meter tall. And he'll be forced into one of those raiding parties. Please . . . please, let's get him down first? Please?"

Pandy just turned her head and looked right into Alcie's green eyes. Then she shook her head as if it were the most obvious thing in the world.

"Duh!"

CHAPTER TWENTY-ONE

Close Call

The heavens, so unbelievably close, cast a gray pall over everything. Even though it was morning, the only light in the village came from the small fires everywhere and the dim sunlight trying desperately to beat its way from the other side of the void, through the blackness, past the stars.

"Why are we going this way?" Alcie asked.

"Because she has to see how the men get into the columns in the first place. We need to go by the big ovens," Iole answered.

The hazy light only confirmed what Pandy had suspected: this small village on the mountaintop was the filthiest place she'd ever seen. People covered in mud and grime, everyone toiling or sleeping; the body stench was overwhelming. Mud pits next to wells next to small ovens next to column bases next to clusters of dozing bodies. There were no roads, just occasional open spaces to jostle in and out of with the rest of the moving throng. The air, which seemed a little cleaner on the climb up the mountain, was once again dense and sooty. The whites of people's eyes, the only clean thing about them, stood out, giving everyone a startled appearance.

Iole led the way through the village. Every few seconds, she would tap her tiny shears defiantly to appease a guard blocking their way or to silence someone demanding to know why they weren't working.

Pandy was deep in thought. What was she going to do to save Homer? It was much easier, she mused, to act on instinct. Since she began her quest, she'd saved others and herself by thinking fast on her feet, or while tied to a chair, or floating in the air. Now that she actually had time to formulate a plan, her insecurities were rising again. She didn't know if she had the brainpower to come up with anything.

Beyond several columns, she saw the building housing her uncle and thought about his fast-growing hair and his tremendous size in comparison with his brother, her father. Her father.

Gods! She hadn't talked to her father in . . . weeks! She looked around. There was so much noise and activity, no one would hear her. And the bottom of the heavens was like a shroud overhead. Zeus could see through the clear skies, but could he see through the darkness of the heavens? Maybe not. She hoped not. And, if anyone stopped them, Iole would need only to wave her little shears and say that Pandy was talking into a shell on "barber business."

Iole was ahead of her and Alcie's eyes were focused on something far in the distance. Slowly, furtively, Pandy reached into her leather carrying pouch, brought out her shell, ran her finger down the lip, and, burying it in her hair, held it to her ear.

Just then, the three of them approached the middle of the village and mixing pit number two.

Prometheus, working at the far end of the pit with Hermes, Amri, and Ismailil, felt his shell vibrate in his cloth sack. Instinctively he reached in and pulled it out.

"Pandy?" he said softly, turning away so as not to attract attention.

"Hi, Daddy," she replied, keeping her voice low.

"Prometheus." Hermes leaned over and spoke softly, "Your girl is heading this way."

Prometheus looked over his shoulder and followed Hermes' gaze. He spotted Pandy, perhaps thirty meters away, slowly wending past a guard hut and the main water well, pushing her way through the crowd. Her hand was hidden in her hair as she pretended to scratch her ear. More than anything else at that moment, he wanted to run and throw his arms around his daughter.

"How's everything at home?" Pandy asked.

"What are you *doing*?" hissed Alcie, her face close by.

"Talking to my dad—don't look at me! Act like this is normal."

"Oh, toasted grape seeds. Puh-leeze."

"Everything is fine, honey," Prometheus said, certain that Xander *was* fine with Sabina, as he watched his daughter approach the mixing pit. "How are you? Uh, where are you?"

"Keep it low, Pro," Hermes cautioned, his eyes on the guard hut.

"I'm on top of Jbel Toubkal. I've seen Uncle Atlas, Dad. I think I know where Laziness is hiding. It's in his nose hair!"

"Yeah, it's pretty big, isn't it?" Prometheus said, then realized his blunder.

"How do you know that, Dad?"

"Uh . . . uh . . ."

He had a single moment to think of his answer, because just then Ismailil and Amri saw Pandy walking toward the mixing pit.

"Pandy! Pandy!" they cried.

Tossing down their mixing poles, they raced around the pit, to the surprise of all the slaves, including Prometheus.

"Well, honey . . . uh . . . ," he said, watching the two little boys throw themselves all over his daughter in a fit of glee. "I know how big my brother is normally, remember? If an evil has gotten in his nose hair, then it must be enormous, right?"

"Pandy!" Amri was yelling and pulling on her cloak.

"Oh, yeah. Duh! That makes sense. Hi, Amri!" Pandy said. Then she became a little disoriented from the clamoring boys and the surrounding din, unsure of which sounds were which. "Hey, Dad, sounds noisy where you are. What's going on in the background?"

Pandy, Alcie, and Iole had stopped directly in front of the mixing pit.

"Uh, that's your brother," Prometheus faltered. "It's uh . . . uh . . ."

"Xander, Dad. His name is Xander."

"What? Oh, yes, it's Xander," Prometheus said, entranced at the happy scene in front of him. Then he saw two huge, sinister-looking Roman guards on the move, heading toward the fuss. He nodded to Hermes, who also took note of the guards and began hurrying, as fast as his old-man body would move, around the side of the pit.

"Where are you? What are you doing with Xander?" she asked into the shell, bending down to ruffle Ismailil's hair. "Hey, Ismailil," she whispered, hugging him tightly as the little boy clung adoringly to her legs.

"Wow," Prometheus said softly, turning his back on the scene again, aware of the fact that the Pandora *he* knew would rather be caught dead than actually be nice to little boys. And these two *knew* her . . . and liked her—no, *loved* her. His daughter had changed.

" 'Wow' what, Dad?" she asked.

"Uh, nothing. Where are we? Uh . . . Xander and I are at a . . . a . . . bake sale. They're trying to rebuild the Athena Maiden Middle School and we brought some of Sabina's, uh, cookies."

"Pandy," Iole said, "we have to keep moving."

"All right, Dad, I have to go," she said, realizing she was causing too much commotion and that people staring was *soooo* not a good thing.

"Me too, honey . . . oh, I love you so much. I'm so proud of you," Prometheus said, looking again over his shoulder. "Big-time phileogottagobye."

He shut off the shell and watched the two guards, now almost upon his daughter.

"Hey, boys, I have to go . . . but I'll be back, okay?" Pandy said to Amri and Ismailil, covertly replacing the shell in her pouch—but not without Amri seeing.

"Were you talking to your father?" Amri asked softly.

Pandy nodded, then winked at him, putting her finger to her lips.

"Pandy," Alcie said, "let's move!"

"All right, little ones," Hermes said, suddenly appearing between Pandy and the boys. "Let's get you back to work!"

"Oh, you're Greek!" Pandy said to the old man.

"By Jupiter, what's going on here?" asked one of the Roman guards, striding up.

"They're with me," Iole said in Latin, pointing to the scissors dangling from her neck.

"Very well," said the guard, "but if you maidens have business here, be quick about it."

"Yes, sir! We're on our way," said Alcie.

"Pandy!" Amri was yelling, reaching out for her with his arms as Hermes ushered him and Ismailil back to the far end of the pit.

"Be good, Amri!" Pandy called after him, then to Hermes, "Thank you, sir!"

"No trouble. My friend and I have just been helping the little brothers with their burden, that's all," said Hermes to Pandy, indicating another ancient man, covered in mud from head to toe, watching her intently from the far end.

"Well, thank you, sir," Pandy said to the second old man, looking at his thin white hair and toothless smile, "they're like my own brothers. Thank you for taking care of them."

Prometheus, unrecognized, nodded feebly at his daughter.

Pandy waved at the boys and moved on.

"She looks good, don't you think?" Hermes whispered, ambling up. "Little more meat on her bones, cheeks flushed . . . looking more like her mother every day. 'Course, she looks a little tired."

"Yeah, she's . . . she's tired," Prometheus choked.

"Aw, come on, pal," Hermes said, putting a withered hand on his friend's shoulder, "don't fall apart on me now. No tears. This is good. She's good."

Prometheus wiped his face and nodded. With a little smile at Hermes, he put his shell back in his pouch.

Amri noticed his movement and, eyes wide, nudged Ismailil. Ismailil turned to look and the brothers saw their new friend, Theus, had a shell *exactly* like the one Pandy had used to talk to her father.

Prometheus then went back to work, completely unaware that both little boys were now staring at him very, very hard.

CHAPTER TWENTY-TWO

The Ovens of Jbel Toubkal

"Atlas's whole idea is to make as many columns as fast as possible," Iole was saying as they trudged toward a particularly hot area of the village. "So he has ovens everywhere on the mountain, but the ones we're heading toward are the biggest."

"I heard this morning, just before my shift ended," Alcie cut in, "that Atlas has finally started the expansion into other areas of the mountain range. He thinks that he's got enough columns around here to hold this section pretty firm . . . I mean, like, in terms of numbers. Now he just needs to keep men in them."

"Doesn't he know he's going to run out of men eventually?" Pandy asked as they passed a large group of the tiny, baked used-men now being trained in the use of tiny swords.

"He doesn't like to think past today, says it's too much work," Iole responded. "That's a direct quote."

They rounded the corner of a long row of makeshift shelters, and in a large clearing, Pandy saw five large ovens, each with an opening at least two meters in diameter. At first the heat shimmer blurred the actual activity, and the tremendous warmth felt like a wonderful bath. But soon Pandy realized she was drenched in her own perspiration. Moving along the side so as to escape the wind generated by the fires, Pandy at last saw what was being done.

On the other side of the clearing, a long row of pre-baked cylindrical column sections extended away from the ovens. Guards were forcing the men, horizontally, into holes in the center of these sections, waist deep, then slaves were packing the remaining spaces with wet mud. Some men were screaming and fighting with all their strength only to be beaten into submission; others were just hanging limply, awaiting their fate.

Then, whenever an oven was free, a cylinder was rolled, slowly, by many slaves, up a wooden ramp and onto a platform, one in front of each oven. These platforms then slid onto a rack, which moved in and out of the oven. Only the clay and mud of each section was placed into the oven; the men remained outside the opening and, as each cylinder was slid inside, a heavy black protective cloth was thrown over the man inside.

The fires were so hot that it took only ten minutes

exactly before the wet mud had been baked hard enough to imprison each man.

"They bake the cylinder, but not the man," Pandy said.

"They have it down to a science," Iole went on, tapping her shears to a curious guard.

"Iole!" said Pandy as a thought struck her. "Why didn't you give Homer the Eye of Horus? He might not feel any effects at all. It might have saved him!"

"Oh, of course! Why didn't we think of that?" Iole said sarcastically.

"I only meant . . . ," Pandy said quickly.

"As if we even knew what was going to happen to him when we were led in here? As if we weren't shackled ourselves and couldn't move! You're certainly not serious, are you?"

"I'm sorry, Iole," Pandy said. "That was stupid of me to even ask."

"We couldn't have done it, duh," Alcie said. "But don't think we didn't think about it. Lemons, I even tried to slip it around his neck when I went up to feed him, but his neck's so thick it won't go around. I found a longer piece of leather and was going to give it to him, but they took him off my rounds yesterday, so I've only been able to see him from far away."

"I'm sorry, guys . . . it was dumb."

"Apology accepted. So is this giving you any ideas of how to get him out?" Iole asked.

"Um, absolutely," Pandy lied.

Without warning, a shout went up.

"Number one, *done!*" a slave called.

Over at the first oven, the black cloth was ripped away, the man underneath gasped for air. The platform was swiveled sideways and the cylinder rolled back onto the ground and away. The whole process began again. Ovens were loaded and unloaded three more times while the girls watched.

"Come on," Pandy said at last, "take me to Homer."

"Ooooh, you've got a plan! I can tell. Iole, she's got a plan!" Alcie squealed, then she yawned widely.

"Oh, Alce, when do you sleep?" Pandy asked.

"I can't sleep," Alcie said. "Not with Homie up there. I try, but I can't shut off my mind."

"Don't say a word," Iole mumbled to Pandy.

They slowly made their way to the far side of the village, passing other wells and mixing pits and prebaking ovens. And everywhere, columns.

"Watch this," Iole said, bringing them to a halt at one point and gesturing to a column and a huge piece of strange equipment nearby.

"What's that?" Pandy said.

"An LPLD," Alcie replied matter-of-factly.

"Once more, in Greek, if you please?" Pandy asked.

"A Large Portable Lifting Device," Alcie said.

"We have no idea what the actual name is," Iole said.

"Alcie came up with LPLD because she's not clever when she's tired."

"I have no problem admitting that," Alcie said with a shrug.

The LPLD was being rolled into position alongside the column. For a second, Pandy was reminded of the scaffolding she would see periodically on the sides of buildings or temples back home when workers needed to repair something high up on the exterior. But this contraption looked more ominous. It was a huge array of beams, boards, ropes, and spinning wheels; the entire device was only slightly taller than the man on the column (almost reaching the very bottom of the heavens).

"It's sort of a pulley," Pandy said.

"That's what I said," Alcie replied. "It's a pulley."

Two slaves raced up two wooden ladders, then transferred onto two ropes hanging down on either side from the top of each column.

"Oh, I get it . . . a regular ladder could never go up that high," Pandy said.

"Well, it could," Alcie said, "but it would be unwieldy."

Pandy looked at her.

"That's what Iole told me."

The slaves, now at the top, each grabbed two hooks from the pulley, dangling in the air close by, and set the hooks into grooves in the top section.

At a signal, slaves manning the ropes lifted the top

section off and lowered it to the ground. Then, just as quickly, the new section with a new slave was lifted high and set into place.

"Raise your arms, slave!" commanded a guard on the ground. Slowly, the man in the new section lifted his arms, the muscles on his back tensing and straining as he began holding up his own little section of the heavens.

"But what about the used-man?" Pandy asked.

"Watch," said Iole.

With picks and hammers, two men began pounding on the hard clay of the old section until it simply crumbled. The used-man fell limply onto the ground, where he was lifted to his feet and led away.

"Why is his bottom half twisted and red?" Pandy asked quietly. "It wasn't exposed."

"That much weight . . . that high up?" Iole said. "I don't think we'll ever know what it must be like. The sun and weight penetrates, I'm certain."

"My Homie is losing his silky smoothness," Alcie said quietly.

"Oh, please," Iole muttered.

"What? I'll still like him!" Alcie said.

Pandy had never really stopped to think about her uncle and what his life had been, and would be again, if she could get Laziness back in the box. She had taken for granted that the heavens would always be far, far overhead. It was just something normal, like Sabina's bad cooking. She hadn't really pondered what strength and courage it took to bear the heavens, *the whole thing*, all alone. She looked up: everywhere around her men were sunk into columns, their arms and backs being twisted and crunched, baked into bizarre, gruesome statues.

The girls continued walking until they were close to the inner wall of the mountain that sloped up to the ridge. An enormous guard stepped directly into their path.

"Why aren't you three working?" he demanded.

"Excuse us," Iole said, tapping her shears. "Out of our way, please."

"What's that? Huh? Okay, so you have a tiny pair of clippy things around your neck, so what? Get back to work!"

"I beg your pardon, sir, but I am assistant to the barbers of Atlas and as such I have been given liberty to traverse this entire village in peace and safety. And they are with me."

"I know nothing about this."

"What are you . . . *new*?" asked Alcie.

"Yes."

"Oh," Iole said, "well, I urge you to ask anyone, and now, if you please."

"I don't think so." The guard grabbed Iole by her arm.

"That arm was recently broken, sir," she said calmly but sternly, "and if you break it again and I am unable to satisfactorily perform my duties, *you will be broken*, sir, *by Atlas himself*!"

"All right, suppose what you say is true," said the guard after a moment, releasing his grasp, "what are you doing out here? And what are these others doing with you?"

Iole hesitated a moment too long.

"Yeah, I thought so," said the guard, grabbing for Iole once more.

"Atlas wants a new look!" Pandy blurted out.

Iole and Alcie just turned to stare at her.

"A what?" asked the guard.

"Yessss," said Pandy, wondering exactly what was coming out of her mouth next, "he's tired of having black hair and he wants to go blond."

"Thaaat's riiiiiight," said Alcie.

"Atlas sent you out here to find a new *hair color*?" the guard asked.

"Precisely," said Iole. "After much research and experimentation, he's decided that the hair color he wants is exactly the same as that of the youth on that column."

She pointed to a column about twenty meters away on the slope. Alcie quickly readjusted Iole's arm to a different column in the same area.

"So we have to bring him in . . . have to get him down," Pandy said.

"So we can match it," Alcie said.

"That's why she's out here," said the guard, nodding

at Iole. "But you two don't have the little clippy things around your necks."

"We're consulting," Pandy said. "I previously worked at Calypso's Clay Pot Beauty Emporium in Athens. I was an expert in color."

"And so was I," said Alcie.

Pandy spied an LPLD being hauled toward a nearby column.

"Ah, perfect! Right on time," she said. "Iole, would you please redirect that pulley toward the . . . column . . . that we need it, uh, under?"

"Certainly," Iole said, running off.

"And since you're here," Pandy continued to the guard, "it would be so helpful if you could supervise."

"I don't know," he said at last, a scowl creeping over his face. "This doesn't sound right. I need to talk to my captain."

"Well, I'm sure he'll say the same," Alcie called after him, but he was already clomping out of sight.

"Sour plums! He's gonna come back and he's gonna be mad!" She whirled on Pandy. "So, Atlas is gonna *dye his hair*? *This* was your big plan?"

"I didn't have a plan!" Pandy cried, racing after Iole and the portable pulley.

"But I thought you had a plan!" yelled Alcie, running to catch up.

"I never had a plan!"

CHAPTER TWENTY-THREE

Homer up High

With Iole directing the slave guard, the LPLD was almost in position underneath Homer's column.

"How are we gonna get him out, huh?" Iole heard Alcie say to Pandy as the two girls caught up.

"I don't know yet," Pandy responded.

"She doesn't have a plan." Alcie smirked at Iole.

"So I surmised," Iole said to Pandy.

Alcie ordered two slaves to help her position the two short ladders.

"We'll get him down and then we'll figure it out," Pandy said, totally unsure of what was going to happen next.

"Come on," Alcie said to Pandy.

Alcie began climbing one ladder while Pandy followed up the second.

"Wait! Oh Gods," Alcie cried when she was only a few meters high. "Hang on . . ."

Alcie fumbled in her pouch for a moment, then withdrew the Eye of Horus on a long leather strand.

"Got it!" she cried.

Alcie rushed up her ladder again, passing Pandy. After only a few meters, they transferred onto the rope ladders hanging from the top. Neither girl spoke until they were almost eighteen meters high. Then Pandy stopped.

"Alce!"

"What's wrong?" Alcie called down.

"I . . . just looked down. I . . . I . . . can't move," Pandy said. Her teeth were chattering a little and her knuckles were turning white as she gripped the ropes.

Alcie descended her rope ladder and leaned out to look Pandy in the eye.

"Look at me. Pandy, look at me! You've been this high up before . . . Olympus, right? The Chamber of Despair in Egypt?"

"I know, but . . . but . . . the ground just kinda rushed away from me," Pandy said, closing her eyes and swaying a tiny bit. "Oh Gods, all I can think about is falling out of Apollo's chariot."

"Okay, right, that was bad. But . . . but . . . you're here! You lived! Figs! Look at me! You can do this. You made it this far without missing a single step, and you're almost there! Now, look at me, right in the eyes . . . good girl . . . now take one step. Just one."

"I can't," Pandy whispered.

"Don't gimme that! Pomegranates. You can do anything. I've seen you! Anything. Except maybe come up with a good plan. Now, with me, one step."

Pandy put her foot on the next rung of the rope ladder, then quickly took it down again.

"Can't."

"Pandy, keep looking at me. Listen, Homer is up there and he is counting on us. On you. On *you*, okay? Now, with me."

Pandy looked at Alcie and didn't move her eyes. Slowly she climbed the next rung.

"Good girl! Okay, let's think about something really great," Alcie said, climbing just a little faster, forcing Pandy to keep up. "Like how much Tiresias the Younger is gonna soooo like you when we get home and he hears about how you saved the world and everything."

"He got . . . t-t-turned into a g-girl, remember?" Pandy said, breathing hard.

"I'm not saying there won't be adjustments. Keep it in the positive! Like with Homie and me. He totally, like, lives in a different city, but we're gonna write and stuff . . ."

"Alcie, Tiresias the Younger is a girl!" Pandy said, climbing without really thinking.

". . . and we're gonna see each other during festivals . . . and here we are!"

Alcie stopped climbing only two meters from the top.

"Not so bad. Okay," she said, "I've seen them do this. Reach out and grab the two hooks closest to you."

Pandy saw the hooks, easily within reach, yet still she closed her eyes as she grabbed for them, horrified of looking down.

"Got 'em?" Alcie asked.

"Wait, yes."

"Good. Now, put the hooks in the two grooves on your side. Don't . . . don't look down! Look at me, if you have to. Are they in?"

"Yes," Pandy said, hooking the second rope.

"Good, now wait a moment before we signal to the ground," Alcie said, climbing higher.

"Hi, Homie," Pandy heard Alcie say. "Pandy's with me and we're gonna get you down. Pandy . . . Pandy, come up here."

Gods, Pandy thought, this was how it was all gonna end. No Hera, no enchantment, no magic. Just a fall off a rope ladder.

"Hi," she said, slowly climbing the last few rungs of the rope ladder to bring herself up to one side of Homer. Then she caught her breath.

Homer's back was almost completely twisted around and his skin, the color of a ripe peach, had tiny wrinkles in most places.

"Hi, Homer," she said again.

But Homer didn't speak; he didn't even acknowledge

219 🔲

they were there. His eyes were shut tight, his mouth was set in a terrible grimace. His breath was coming in short, sharp bursts. Pandy saw the darkness over his head, huge stars once again so close by, and Homer's hands pressing on something transparent.

"Okay, Homie, we're gonna lift you off. Here, take this," Alcie said, placing the Eye of Horus around Homer's neck. Almost immediately, Pandy noticed Homer's eyes and jaw relax just the tiniest bit, although he was still silent.

"We're gonna signal now," Alcie said to Homer, reaching up to quickly stroke his cheek. "So when I tell you, drop your arms and duck your head. Pandy, back down the ladder a bit. You're gonna be okay, Homie."

As they descended several meters on the rope ladders, Alcie waved her arms. The top of the pulley was moved in directly over Homer's head, the metal rods and wheels just brushing the bottom of the heavens; slowly the ropes were drawn taut over the metal wheels and the top section began to lift off.

"Okay, Homie, drop it!" Alcie cried, and Homer lowered his arms and hung his head.

"Stop at once!" came a distant shout.

At that instant, Pandy and Alcie spied the guard, returning with his captain . . . and one of the barbers.

There was some confusion on the ground, and the slaves stopped lifting for a second.

"I said stop!" came the cry again, but the guards and the barber were still out of sight to those on the ground.

Pandy saw Iole run to the slave guard and start speaking very fast, clutching her tiny shears. The guard motioned to the slaves and they began lifting the section again. Now the pulley swiveled outward, dangling the section twenty meters above the ground.

"Gods, they're coming back! Should we try to bring him toward us?" Alcie said, panicking.

"No! We can't do it, Alce. We can't reach the section," Pandy replied.

The slaves began lowering the section to the ground as Homer hung limply over the side. As he passed Alcie and Pandy, he managed to look up and smile weakly.

"Stop this now!"

Suddenly, the section jerked to a halt as the approaching guards met the group of slaves. Without thinking, Pandy and Alcie raced as fast as their legs would take them to the bottom of the rope ladders, then they scurried down the wooden ladders.

"Who gave the order to do this?" a different guard, young but with white hair, asked the slave guard.

"That one," the slave guard said, pointing to Iole.

"What gives you the authority?" said the white-haired guard, advancing on Iole.

"This does," she spoke defiantly, unaware of the

barber heading toward her. "We're on a mission for Atlas by direct order of his barbers."

"What mission is this?" said the barber, striding up. "I gave you an order, did I? What order did I give you that I cannot remember? Hmmm?"

"Uh, you asked me . . . don't you recall?" Iole looked like she was going to be ill.

"This youth isn't scheduled to be removed until tonight." The white-haired guard was now forcing Iole backward toward the base of the pulley. "What makes you so interested in him?"

"His hair," Iole sputtered.

"I told you *nothing* about his hair or anything else, you worthless girl!" screamed the barber.

"Put him back!" yelled the guard to the slaves. "He serves his full time!"

As the slaves began to twist and pull at the ropes, maneuvering Homer's section back onto the column, Alcie, standing in the shadow of the column, grabbed Pandy's arm.

"Oh Gods . . . Pandy, what do we do?"

"This is what we do," Pandy said softly, and trained her eyes on one of the ropes. At once, a fine stream of smoke began rising as individual fibers began to char.

"If I can just cut through one," she said to Alcie, her irises fading, her eyes going white, "then, I think, he'll lower to the ground. The slaves won't be able to hold him."

"Oh, sweet nectarines." Alcie shifted her gaze back and forth from Homer to Pandy's eyes.

The white-haired guard was still advancing on Iole, his sword now drawn.

"You're a troublemaker, you are. I have no idea what little scheme you and your friends are trying to pull off, but I have complete authority to deal with troublemakers as I see fit."

Pop!

The rope burned through and snapped, causing the slaves holding it to fall backward. One of the hooks fell loose and went hurtling to the ground. Homer was grabbing as hard as he could on to two ropes, preventing the section from toppling away from the three other hooks.

The weight was too much for the slaves on the remaining ropes; they began lowering Homer.

Iole was now pinned against the base of the pulley as the white-haired guard raised his sword. His eyes flicked for an instant over the broken rope.

"Was that part of it, huh? Disable the pulleys one by one? You're working against Atlas? Why, I wonder. No matter, I'll get that information from the other two. Do I have your blessing, barber?" he asked, not taking his eyes off Iole's face.

"You most certainly do. She's a liar . . . and replaceable!" yelled the barber.

The white-haired guard sent his sword whistling through the air toward Iole's head. Iole, at the very last second, unexpectedly dove to the ground, sending the sword right into the ropes. The sword sliced cleanly through one rope, scattering the slaves holding on to it and sending Homer's section plummeting to the earth.

Alcie screamed. The slaves screamed. The guards yelled and shoved each other out of the way; one guard pushed another into the barber, who was then propelled, screaming, directly underneath the falling hunk of baked clay. The only one who didn't scream was Pandy. Looking up, she flash heated the two whirring metal pulley wheels to a point where they became gummy without becoming liquid. As she took her gaze away, the sticky metal caught the ropes and slowed the section down enough that it landed, intact, roughly but safely.

Everyone stared at Homer (and two feet wearing Persian slippers sticking out from under the hard clay). No one moved for a second and that was all it took for the section to topple onto its side, exposing the barber (now flat as a papyrus sheet) and flinging the still-weak Homer about like a rag doll, who then began to roll down the slope and into the village.

CHAPTER TWENTY-FOUR
Homer on a Roll

As the section of column headed down the slope, it rapidly began to pick up speed. Somehow it missed hitting every other standing column in the area, which might have slowed it a little. Instead, with nothing in its way and the speed increasing, Pandy knew that when it finally *did* hit something, whatever it hit *and* Homer were both going to be shattered.

"Gods!" Pandy cried, watching the section bounce down the slope.

"Tanger*INES*!" Alcie screamed as she took off after Homer. Pandy and Iole also took advantage of the disorder around them and, escaping the astounded guards, ran after Alcie.

Because it was much heavier at one end, the section was rolling fast in a wide arc directly through the main part of the village. People glanced up from their tasks at the screams and commotion on the hillside, then scattered like birds as Homer came crashing toward them.

Oddly enough, the first thought that went through Homer's mind as he started to roll downhill was not how hard the ground was each time his head hit it, but how good it felt to have the use of his arms back again. His mind, now free from trying to distract itself from the pain of bearing the heavens, snapped into focus. Quickly, Homer gathered loose rope ladders, which were flying out behind the section, whipping in all directions like snapping snakes. Holding the ropes and bringing his arms around his head, he formed a protective rope cocoon, which built on itself with every rotation, and which held him somewhat steady, although he couldn't see anything but a spinning blur. He was sure he should be nauseated, but then he remembered the Eye of Horus. And then he knocked his head on a stray water bucket and passed out.

Men dove into mud pits, women hid behind ovens or tottered on the edges of water wells, a chicken flew all of two meters and landed on a guard's helmet. A dog ran after the rolling column, barking ferociously.

Several guards, standing by a well, tried to stop the section: one had his foot mangled and another lost two fingers, but that contact was enough to skew the course of the arc and cause the section to just miss getting bogged down in mixing pit number two.

Prometheus and Hermes looked up from mixing in time to see Homer go hurtling by. Then, less than ten seconds later, Alcie, Pandy, and Iole raced after it, followed by a dozen or so guards . . . then everyone in the village who'd seen the spectacle.

Dropping their poles, Prometheus, Hermes, Amri, and Ismailil dashed into the flowing river of bodies, trying to keep an eye on the rolling column and the girls, but it wasn't two seconds before Prometheus heard Ismailil yell. The boys were too little to keep pace and had fallen to the ground, in danger of being trampled.

"Hermes!" shouted Prometheus, not caring at all who heard.

Hermes turned back, saw the boys in the dirt, and with a flick of his wrist, gently parted the crowd, forming a narrow but clear path. In no time they were gaining on Iole, then Pandy, then Alcie, who was running and screaming at the same time.

"Nectarines, get out of my way! Homie! Apples . . . apples, move! Fiiiiiigs!"

"Iole," Pandy cried, seeing the crowd fleeing, "look where he's headed!"

"I see it!" Iole yelled back. "He's gonna be smashed to bits!"

The arc of the section, having missed everything else in the village, was now taking Homer directly toward the building inside which sat her uncle Atlas. In less than five seconds, Homer would crash right into one of the thick outer walls.

"Homie!" Alcie screamed. "Noooooo!"

The section rolled up a discarded ramp from a nearby oven and was airborne for the last few meters.

Then Homer hit the wall.

With a deafening explosion, the wall blew apart, forcing the two adjoining walls to crumble with a roar. A large section of the roof at the shattered end came crashing down, driving clouds of dust up and out. People everywhere screamed, blinded and choking, falling all over themselves. Even the guards, normally so sinister and controlling, ran in terror or just stood gaping.

Alcie didn't falter; she ran headlong into the dust and right up over the rubble calling Homer's name. Pandy and Iole followed her into the chaos, picking their way over the debris, but stopped when they came upon Alcie, standing on a chunk of wall, staring straight ahead.

The section carrying Homer had come to a full stop at last. Still intact.

Right at the feet of Atlas, who had been napping but was now wide-awake.

And angry.

CHAPTER TWENTY-FIVE

Swingin'

Fortunately, and unusually, the building had been almost empty. There were no lines of slaves and no guards waiting in groups off to the side. With nothing to do, Atlas's two main henchmen had slipped out the back to eat a few lotus leaves. The explosion behind them so startled one that he turned too fast and butted heads with his comrade, knocking them both out cold. In fact, the only one in the building was Atlas himself.

With no one to prod him gently, he was startled awake and slightly confused, which always made him angry.

Seeing the far end of the building blown out, the roof caved in, and three young girls standing on top of the rubble amidst the whirling dust, his first instinct was to kick out or grab on to something hard and real.

He saw the section of column at his feet with a cluster of rope at one end, and raised his foot to stomp down on it with all the force he could muster.

Alcie screamed at the same time Pandy yelled, "You don't want to do that!"

Atlas paused, his foot in midair.

"Uh, I don't think you want to do that," Pandy yelled again.

Atlas was unaccustomed to being spoken to in such a tone. He cocked his enormous head to one side and stared at Pandy.

"Yes I do," he said at last. It was in that second that Pandy realized she was dealing with a gigantic baby.

"No, you really, really don't," Pandy said.

"I don't?"

"No way."

"Why not?"

Pandy got a little closer to her uncle. She noticed at once that his mutant nose hair, in only the few hours that she'd been in the village, had grown to a length of almost a meter and a half and was now very thick and riddled with rust red veins. She quickly took off her leather carrying pouch.

"Hold this," she said quietly, handing it to Iole and climbing down off the rubble toward Atlas. "Uh, you don't want to do that because . . . because . . . what you really want to do is . . . is . . . find out what just happened to your hut, home . . . place! I mean, just look around. What *is* all this? You don't know, right?"

"Right!" Atlas said. "What happened?"

"Why don't you put your foot down and I'll tell you," Pandy said, an idea percolating. She knew the hair with Laziness had to be pulled out at the root, and if she could just get close enough to his nose to grab hold . . .

Atlas lowered his leg, but his big toe bumped the column section slightly. That was all it took to shatter the hard clay. The section fell away, revealing Homer's lower half. His toga was dirty and brown, but his legs were perfect.

"What's this?" Atlas asked, bending to peer at Homer, still unconscious underneath the rope cocoon. "Is this the cause?"

"No," said Pandy as she approached, watching Atlas's nose hair drag on the ground as he bent his head. She began wiping her hands on her toga, drying them to get a good grip. "It was your . . . your . . . guards. They're trying to take over!"

She was two meters from his face; still too far to jump for it.

"They're trying to kill you!" Alcie cried from behind her.

Pandy took one more step and was within striking distance. She leapt forward, hands ready to clutch the thick, ugly hair, when Atlas suddenly rose to his feet to tower above her.

"They are? My guards are trying to kill me?" he yelled.

Pandy landed right on top of Homer's stomach, which made Homer twitch and groan ever so slightly. She looked up at her uncle, thinking he hadn't seemed so large when he was just sitting down, but now he was almost ten meters high.

And then, as Pandy stared in shock, he grew *again*. His legs stretched several more meters as did his arms, and his torso expanded in all directions. Even his head grew bigger. Only seconds later, Atlas was at his full height, bursting through the remaining roof and standing erect, almost eighteen meters tall, just arm's distance from the bottom of the heavens.

"I see I need to smash some heads," Atlas said. "Somebody's going off the mountain!"

"Wait!" Pandy cried, picking herself up. "You don't know which ones they are!"

"Doesn't matter," Atlas said, beginning to move. "First one I see goes off the mountain!"

With one step, Atlas strode over the broken heap of wall and out into the crowd. Thousands of people, none of whom had ever seen a Titan at full height, fled in every direction. Atlas grabbed the first two guards he came upon and began clomping toward the nearest ridge.

Pandy raced over the rubble, passing Alcie, who was heading toward Homer.

"I'll stay with him, you and Iole go!"

Pandy and Iole sped into the crowd, now less dense, and chased after Atlas. Within only a minute they found they were almost upon him.

"That makes no sense," Iole panted as she and Pandy dashed off to the side to parallel the Titan's course. "He should be at the edge of the mountain by now!"

"No," Pandy heaved, watching her uncle carefully, "look at him! He's trying not to step on anybody!"

"Great Athena," Iole said.

It was true. Atlas was almost tottering on his gargantuan legs, looking all around him, and taking teensy steps in an effort not to trample any workers. And he was apologizing to everyone.

"Sorry. Pardon me. Sorry. Have to kill some guards. Excuse me. Oooh, was that your baby? No? Baby's okay? Good. Excuse me. Pardon me, please."

Pandy and Iole stopped for a moment to watch the spectacle, doubled over in hysterics. Then, out of nowhere, Pandy grabbed Iole's arm, a picture forming in her mind.

"Come on," she cried, sprinting forward, "I have to get on top of the ridge before he does."

She and Iole wove a tight course through the village, much of which was now fairly deserted, as most of the crowd was behind them and running the other way. The girls were unaware of the two old men doggedly following them. The closest ridge was in sight, empty of guards;

they had all abandoned their posts at the first sign of trouble in the village. Pandy and Iole passed the last column and started up the slope. Cresting the ridge, Pandy almost sailed over the sheer drop on the other side, flailing her arms wildly as she teetered on the edge. Just as she was about to go over, Iole thrust out her arm and grabbed a handful of Pandy's toga, yanking Pandy back and pulling herself up as well.

"Thank you," Pandy said.

"My pleasure," Iole replied. "Now, you probably don't have a plan . . ."

"Shhhhh! Hang on," Pandy said, silencing Iole and watching Atlas approach the ridge. He would land on the crest only fifteen meters away, just past a large cluster of boulders. Pandy turned to Iole.

"I have a plan."

"Naturally." Iole grinned.

Prometheus had to stop for a moment. Panting heavily, he leaned on an oven, now cooling with no one tending the dying fire. Hermes, on his spindly old-man legs, strode up right beside him, perfectly rested, not a white hair out of place.

"Did you have to make me *feel* old? Couldn't you just have made me *look* old?" Prometheus gasped.

"Absolutely. But where's the fun?"

"So . . . now we'll save her, right?"

"No," Hermes said.

"*No?* What do you mean, no?"

"I mean, my friend, if she gets killed, she gets killed. We'll both know the Fates decreed it. To completely prevent her from being killed would have required interceding with the Fates. That means forms in triplicate, signatures, briberies, and playing footsie with Clotho, if you know what I'm saying, and I am just not up to that."

"But you promised."

"No such thing did I do."

"Then why did you bring me, Hermes? You're a joker, but you're not cruel."

"No, I'm not," Hermes said, calmly watching Pandy almost fall off the side of the mountain in the distance. "I brought you because you got on your knees. You'd never do that for anyone or anything unless your heart and soul were on the line. Since recapturing this particular evil has now become a family matter, I felt you should see the outcome for yourself; you need to know the facts of what's going to happen with your daughter and your brother. That's why I brought you."

"I'm still gonna save her if she needs saving," Prometheus said, ambling off toward the ridge with a glare at Hermes.

"You can try, my friend," Hermes sighed to himself, walking slowly behind. "You can try,"

Pandy and Iole raced across the ridge and hid themselves behind two of the largest boulders just as Atlas started up the slope. He was moving faster now; no people to mind underfoot. Pandy poked her head up from her hiding place, knowing she would have to time her movements to the second.

In one stride, Atlas was halfway up the slope. As he took his next step, he bent forward to steady himself, bringing his head low to the ground, just below the crest. In that second, before he brought his other leg up, Pandy bolted from behind the rocks and shot herself forward and up, arms outstretched, aiming straight for the huge nose hair.

And in that second she realized that she was about to grab it with her bare hands. She'd already been infected by Jealousy and Vanity by mistakenly touching them. Why didn't she think about Laziness!? What would this do to her? And how could she have been so stupid to forget the adamant *net*!

Clomp.

Suddenly she had the hair in both hands and was fifteen meters in the air, hanging on for dear life. Up close, the hair was even more disgusting than she'd imagined;

it was rough all over with its own fuzzy gray hairs and had a stench like burned wood.

Atlas felt a tug on his precious hair and looked down to see Pandy swinging from side to side, like a pendulum, in front of his body. He let out a tremendous, ear-splitting roar and arched his back, flinging his arms out to both sides. He dropped both guards, unconscious, on the slope and began swiping furiously at Pandy. But his movements were clumsy, like those of an infant, and instead of grabbing for her, he was trying to knock her off the hair.

Pandy was not feeling Lazy in the slightest but had no time to wonder why. She was bouncing off the back of Atlas's hands, whipping around to the sides of his neck and caroming off his chest. Suddenly her feet landed on his body and she took that moment to lift up and then give a mighty tug on the root of the hair. Atlas screamed and swung his torso from side to side. In one step he crested the ridge, his head scraping the bottom of the heavens, his cries echoing off the surrounding mountains. Pandy, who had frozen in a fear of heights on the rope ladder only a short time before, was now swinging free over the sheer drop off Jbel Toubkal, certain death thousands and thousands of meters below.

Prometheus was halfway up the slope when his stamina and strength finally gave out. He dropped like a stone to the ground and lay there, heaving, just as Hermes wandered up and sat beside him, and just as Pandy flew onto Atlas's nose hair.

"Please," he whispered to Hermes.

"No," Hermes replied, looking at his dear friend with a small touch of sympathy.

"I . . . hate . . . you," Prometheus said.

"You don't."

"I . . . do."

"If I thought you meant it, I'd be hurt," Hermes said, smiling. "You're the one who wanted the old man disguise."

"But . . ."

"Hush, pal," Hermes said, looking at Atlas standing on the ridge and Pandy clinging to his nose hair, swinging high over the edge. "It's time to watch your girl."

Pandy swung free of Atlas's hands and landed again on Atlas's upper arm. Planting her feet and lifting, she tugged sideways. The hair didn't budge, which, Pandy realized, was a very good thing, because if it had come loose, she would have fallen to her death off the mountain.

Atlas, seeing that his attempts to swat the girl away were doing no good, finally decided to grab at her. Pandy saw his arm stretch wide, his massive palm turn toward her, and knew she had two choices. Either hang on tight to the hair and let him grab her, so that when he yanked her, he'd yank out the hair, too. Or escape being killed by making herself untouchable. She had no desire to be crushed completely, and she knew she couldn't focus the heat directly on his hands, he needed them to hold up the heavens, so she concentrated her power . . . on herself.

She had no idea if it would work, but she directed her power over fire inward and then sent it radiating outward to her skin. As Atlas's hand bore down upon her, she focused everything she had solely on making her skin, and only her skin, hot . . . very hot. So hot that her sandals began to smoke and the bottom of her cloak caught fire. As the complete loss of sound hit her again, she looked at her arms: they were glowing with the radiance of the sun. Atlas's hand closed around her for a moment (which extinguished her cloak), then he roared again and threw his hand back, a small blister on his palm. Pandy felt the nose hair begin to melt slightly where she touched it and reached higher for a better grip, focusing on cutting off the heat to her hands. Atlas whipped his body around as Pandy planted her feet on his chest and tugged again. The hair remained fixed in his nostril, but Pandy lost her footing and slammed into Atlas's chest. She seared his skin, making it bubble, and caused Atlas to stumble forward. He completely lost his balance and tumbled forward in a sideways roll, which whipped Pandy into the ground, almost knocking her out.

Then Atlas slid the last few meters feetfirst, dragging Pandy behind him in the dirt.

He crashed into the closest column, which caused a chain reaction as sections burst apart, smashing into other columns close by. In less than a minute, seventeen columns crashed to the ground.

The sections that hit Atlas's body only glanced off, but the top section, with the slave in it, hit him in just the right soft spot in the middle of his forehead, dazing Atlas to the point that he just lay on the ground, very confused. Pandy stumbled over to her uncle, only somewhat aware of Iole racing down the slope toward her. She clambered onto Atlas's torso, causing the Titan to moan in pain with her every move, and walked over his great barrel chest and thick neck until she was right below his chin. Taking the hair in her hands, Pandy said a short prayer to all the Olympians at once and pulled with all her might. She was unaware that the residual heat from her body was charging up through the hair to its root, causing the skin around it to expand; in fact, now that she was standing so close, Atlas's entire face was turning beet red and his already massive pores were expanding with sweat.

She had used almost all the strength she had and was just starting to realize that it was not going to be enough when . . .

Pop.

The mutant hair flew out of Atlas's nose like a rock out of a slingshot, sailed past Pandy's face, whipped out of her hands, and stuck in the dirt almost five meters away.

Immediately, Pandy felt Atlas's body go limp and saw his head roll to one side. Pandy leapt off Atlas's chest as Iole ran up, the small wooden box already held tight in her hand.

"Ready?" Pandy asked.

"Ready," Iole said.

The two girls dashed off to find the end of the hair.

"Well, Achilles' tendon!" Iole said when they came upon the bulbous mass, now covered with dirt. "No wonder you had such a hard time getting Laziness out."

"The hair itself isn't Laziness," Pandy said. "I grabbed it and . . . nothing. It's concentrated—it's all right at the end."

"You forgot the net, you know," Iole said.

"Thank you, Miss Obvious!"

The end of the hair was at least three times the thickness of the hair itself. It was, under the dirt, milky gray and looked like a large, filmy, slimy rope that had been wound around the end of a stick.

"Looks like the things my dad uses to clean out his ears, only bigger," Pandy said.

"Oh, too much information!" Iole said.

"What*ever*," Pandy said. "Let's just pull it off and get it in the box. Net, please."

Iole fished out the adamant net from Pandy's pouch and handed it over. Then Iole slid Pandy's hairpin out of the clasp on the wooden box and readied herself to open the lid when Pandy gave the order. Pandy wrapped her right hand in the net and moved toward the bulbous mass. Instantly, the sickening gray matter began pulsating, as if it had a heartbeat.

"Not expecting that," Iole said.

"Fine, so it's . . . alive," Pandy said. "Fine."

She was almost upon it when the slimy strand began to uncoil itself from around the hair.

"Gods!" Pandy cried, stepping back. "It's a . . . it's a . . . what *is* it?"

Suddenly, as one end fell to the ground, a large mouth opened up, revealing many rings of sharp gray teeth. Then, just as quickly, the mouth closed up again.

"Incredible!" Iole said, the wooden box dropping to one side. "It's a parasite!"

"What?"

"Makes perfect sense!" Iole gasped. "Laziness was feeding off your uncle, sapping his strength and energy while it lived in his nose."

"Too much information!" Pandy yelled.

The parasite, Laziness, was now fully uncoiled, stretching itself along the ground almost half a meter. At once, the sickly creature began slithering away in the dirt.

"Oh, no you don't!" yelled Pandy, reaching out with the net, but the parasite was too quick and was slithering faster than she could move. Pandy and Iole took off at a run, but the parasite was easily outstripping them, and soon they were out of the area of crashed columns and heading back toward the middle of the village. Workers had begun to filter back from other parts of the village and Laziness was heading right for the middle of a crowd, which included Ismailil and Amri.

"Move, boys, move!" Pandy screamed. "Run!"

The entire crowd scattered again, but the parasite had locked in on Ismailil and was slithering fast, gaining on the little boy. Pandy knew she couldn't zap it with heat; Laziness would vaporize and escape completely. Her only hope was to outrun it, but Laziness was still outmaneuvering Pandy and was now within striking distance of Ismailil, its back end whipping wildly, propelling itself forward.

Just as Laziness was literally rearing its front end, mouth open wide, to attack the little boy, a mixing pole came whistling through the air, caught the parasite in the middle, lifted it high and brought it down again on the ground with a tremendous wallop, pinning Laziness to the earth.

The parasite struggled to free itself, wiggling furiously,

but by then Pandy was upon it, wrapping both hands in the net and grabbing each end.

"I've got it!" she cried, not looking up. The pole was quickly taken away. "Iole?"

"Right here!" she said, gently flipping the clasp on the box.

Laziness was now curling itself like a snake into a tight ball.

"On a count of three—one . . . two . . . *three*!"

Iole cracked the lid just enough and Pandy flung Laziness inside. Iole snapped the lid shut, flipped the clasp down, and slid the hairpin neatly back into place.

"Nicely done," Pandy said to Iole. "I didn't even see anything else try to escape."

"We're getting faster. We should start timing ourselves." Iole smiled back. They both heard the faint hissing as Laziness dissolved inside the box.

Only then did Pandy and Iole both look up to see who had wielded the mixing pole with such force and accuracy. What they saw, however, was a flutter of a dirty cloak as whoever it was was swallowed up in the crowd.

CHAPTER TWENTY-SIX
Brother to Brother

"You told me you were going to the lavatorium!" Hermes said, dragging Prometheus behind a deserted guard hut, away from the crowd. " 'Oh, please, my friend, just give me a little of my strength back so I can hurry to the lavatorium.' That's what you said!"

"I know," Prometheus replied. "And I went. And I also just happened to assist my daughter. I didn't plan it, it just sort of happened."

"You lied."

"Oh, knock it *off* already, would you?" Prometheus cried, startling Hermes. "I have been good as gold—did and didn't do everything you said. Kept my word, didn't let her know I was here, did not interfere with her and Atlas, *as promised*. Watched my baby girl swingin' on the end of his nose hair, almost getting herself killed. Listening to you, just sitting right next to me, relaxed and cool as a cucumber. Blah, blah. Not even caring. And when everything between the two of them was over, done, finished, I just whacked a big . . . whatever it was . . . with a stick. So chain me up in Tartarus now, if you're gonna do it, because if not, I have to go talk to my little brother."

Prometheus began to walk away. After several steps, he stopped and turned around. Hermes was staring at him, mouth agape.

"You coming?" Prometheus asked.

Before Pandy could even rise to follow the person in the cloak, Alcie arrived, trying as best she could to support a very weak Homer.

"We saw it!" Alcie said, sitting Homer down and propping him up against a nearby column. "You okay, Homer?"

"I'm cool," he whispered.

"We saw everything! Well, apricots, almost . . . but we were far away," Alcie said, standing and hugging Pandy. "Gods! For someone who doesn't like heights, you were practically flying off the mountain!"

"Don't remind me, okay?" Pandy said.

"All right," Iole said, "what now?"

"Now," Pandy said, "you guys get some people together and start helping the slaves who crashed down out of the columns. See if Atlas hurt anybody else. I'm gonna—"

"You are going to do nothing, my pretty maiden," a

voice behind her said. Suddenly, Pandy felt herself being shackled into manacles. The brutish guard had hold of her arms as the sinister white-haired guard walked around to face her. Behind him, guards seized Alcie and Iole and put them in chains. Almost every guard in the village was surrounding them in a giant ring.

"This is going to be so much fun for me," the white-haired guard sneered. "For all of us, actually. You arrive and we have nothing but trouble. I just can't decide what to do with you three first. But I know where you're going to end up."

He looked overhead.

"The first maidens to hold the heavens. What an honor!"

The guard spun around to face the crowd.

"Back to work, everybody!" he yelled.

Nobody moved.

"Did you not hear me?" he screamed. "You want to die along with these three? *Get moving!*"

But nobody moved.

They were all looking at the brown-haired girl with the smoking wrists.

"Whaaa?" said the guard softly.

Pandy's head was down, her eyes hidden. The locks on her manacles were glowing bright red and smoking. As they melted off her wrists, she looked up and everyone saw her clear white eyes.

"I so don't think so."

The guards began to flee to the opposite side of the village. Pandy focused her mind on superheating every piece of metal the guards had on them. Immediately, glowing red swords, spears, helmets, cloak pins, shin and wrist guards, and breastplates were flying everywhere. Then she focused on superheating their outer clothing. Suddenly, large men, screaming and wearing nothing but skimpy undertogas, were dashing across the village, away from the enchanted girl.

Pandy took a deep breath and looked at Alcie and Iole, her eyes brown once more.

"You're so cool," Alcie said.

"Thanks." Pandy smiled. "Okay, so you guys get some people—"

"Excuse me, oh cool one." Iole held up her hands, in shackles. "You forgot these."

"Oh, sorry," Pandy said. "Where's the key?"

"Doesn't matter," Iole answered, "it's melted."

"This is so un-cool," Alcie said.

Pandy put her face in her hands.

"Gods!" she groaned into her palms. "I can't melt them off you without burning you."

"No, thank you!" Alcie said. "As if!"

"But I have to go back and talk to my uncle before too much time passes!"

"Look," Iole sighed, "just go. We can deal with these later. Homer's getting his strength back and these shackles aren't even adamant. Maybe he can break them. Just go."

"Okay, I'll be right back. I hope," Pandy said, dashing off, calling back over her shoulder. "I'm sorry!"

Prometheus had been standing beside his brother's giant face for almost a minute, gently poking Atlas's nose with his foot and watching the hairs on Atlas's face and head start to recede and thin out to normal.

"Brother?" he said to the Titan, still unconscious. "Brother? Time to wake up!"

Atlas began to stir. He opened his large eyes, his vision trying to clear. At last, he focused on a tiny old man kicking his nose. As Atlas's brow began to furrow, Prometheus realized the situation.

"Hermes, he doesn't know who I am. Change me back to me."

"Nothing doing, pal," Hermes said, leaning against a shattered column and tossing a hand-sized chunk of clay in the air.

"I'll cover my head with my hood, just do it . . . just until I'm done talking to him."

Hermes looked at Prometheus for a moment, then sighed and flicked his wrist.

Instantly, Prometheus felt himself back in his own body. Covering his head, he peered out from under the hood.

"Atlas?" he said again to the Titan. "Hey, it's me, Brother! It's Prometheus."

"Heeeeyyyy, Prometheus!" Atlas said, still groggy. "What's up? My head hurts!"

"Listen, I don't have time to fill you in on all the details, but you have to pick up the heavens again."

"Huh?" Atlas opened his eyes wide and stared straight up. "Oh, wow! Look at that! There they are! And there are tiny people holding them up. That's cute! Really, really nice!"

"Atlas," Prometheus said, "it's your job. Not theirs. You have to do this."

"No way," Atlas said, closing his eyes. "My head hurts, but my back hasn't felt this good in eons. If they wanna do it, let 'em!"

"They *don't* want to do it and they can't do it. Only you. You forced them and they're being crushed. They're carrying out your punishment!"

"I haaaaaate Zeus," Atlas whined.

"Atlas, pay attention!" Prometheus cried. "You took an oath! You promised. The Titans lost the battle with the Olympians and this is your fate!"

"Fuggedaboutit," Atlas whispered.

Prometheus hung his head, absolutely lost as to what

to say. If his brother didn't want to carry the heavens, there was no way he was going to force him. Only Zeus could intervene, and then Zeus would find out that Prometheus had been on Jbel Toubkal in the first place and that would spell big trouble.

Suddenly, Prometheus was struck with an idea.

"Fine," he said at last. "I could talk about honor . . . and . . . your responsibility, your word, and what you're doing to the world. But I won't."

"Good," Atlas sighed.

"Instead, I'll just say this . . ."

He bent down and whispered into his brother's ear. Atlas began to whimper. Then his eyes shot wide open. Still Prometheus continued to whisper. Finally, Atlas gave a tremendous cry, which Pandy heard as she was picking her way through the column rubble.

"No!" Atlas yelled, sitting up, staring at Prometheus.

Prometheus only nodded solemnly at his brother.

Atlas got to his feet.

"Fine!" he cried, and stomped back into the village just as Pandy rounded a pile of column sections. Prometheus looked at Hermes and instantly felt himself back in the disguise of the old man.

"What happened?" Pandy asked the two old men. "Where is Atlas going?"

"He's off to take up his burden once more," said the one without teeth.

"You're kidding!" Pandy said. "I mean, that was easy. Or was it? What did you say to him?"

"I simply reminded him of his oath to bear the heavens . . . and that if his word meant nothing, his nobility as a great Titan was also worth nothing, and mankind would perish."

"And that worked?" Pandy said, incredulous. "Well, obviously it worked."

"Well, that's what anyone would have said," the old man answered. "That's what *you* would have said, right?"

"Uh . . . yeah," Pandy replied. "Yes, that's exactly what I would have said."

"You'd better hurry if you want to see him do it," said the old man. "You probably won't get another chance, hopefully, and it's rather spectacular. Uh, at least, I think it *must* be. Hurry now."

"Yeah," Pandy said, staring at the old man, something familiar in his . . . voice? . . . eyes? What? Stupid, she thought, couldn't be anything. She'd never met him before that morning.

"Thank you," she said, taking off toward Atlas's hut. "Thanks again!"

Prometheus watched his daughter until she was out of sight, unaware that Hermes had moved beside him.

"Our work here is done," said the god.

"Right," said Prometheus, "let's go home."

CHAPTER TWENTY-SEVEN

Lift and Separate

Pandy saw Atlas towering over the village, standing close to his shattered hut and staring up at the heavens. Trying to keep him in sight as she picked her way through a confused, scattering crowd, she was aware of many fights breaking out between gangs of ex-slaves and near-naked ex-guards. Some people were trying to load the more brutish guards into ovens as others blocked their way, claiming they could not be so harsh in kind. She caused any fire or lit oven she saw to die instantly. She dodged falling chunks of hardened clay as people drove LPLDs into columns willy-nilly, and she stopped to help one elderly woman out of a mixing pit into which she'd been pushed by the rioting crowd.

As Pandy searched the throng for Alcie, Iole, and Homer, she glanced at the narrow pathway leading up and out of the village, now jammed with people hurrying to escape the chaos, most unaware of what was about to happen.

Keeping her uncle in view, she saw Atlas bend down to do something out of sight on the ground. Seconds later, clouds of dust filled the air. As he rose to full height again, Pandy suddenly saw him begin to shake his arms and head wildly from side to side, the way she'd seen members of the Apollo Youth Academy wrestling team warm up before a match, as if he was loosening his muscles. The crowd, however, took these actions as a sign of increasing anger and violence and became more frenzied.

As she neared her uncle, rounding the back of the barbers' hut, the crowd became so thick and riotous that she grabbed the ladder leaning against the hut and clambered up onto the roof. Looking down she saw Ghida, Amri, and Ismailil being swept along with the crowd like leaves in a wild river: Ghida was having trouble keeping the two little boys upright. Frantically, Pandy screamed down at them. It was Ismailil who heard her and saw her gesturing for them to climb the ladder. After all three had joined her on the roof, Pandy and Ghida hauled the ladder up so no one else could use it. There was no sign of Homer, Alcie, and Iole. Pandy scanned the area in front of her uncle: apparently he'd completely cleared the two large platforms where his hut and the cooking hut had once stood. Particles of dust and debris still clouded the air.

Suddenly, Atlas let out a fearful yell, which halted and silenced the entire village. All eyes turned upward.

Amri began to whimper, but Ghida put her arm around him and Pandy whispered in his ear.

"Just watch, okay?"

He stifled a cry, his eyes huge, and nodded to her.

As everyone gaped, Atlas slowly grew another ten meters, hunching his back and shoulders against the bottom of the heavens. He raised his right foot and brought it down squarely on one platform, then brought his left foot down on the other, causing the mountain to tremble. He vigorously rubbed his enormous palms together, turned them upward, and placed them against the heavens. He looked about for a long time and sighed. Then Atlas closed his eyes and took a deep breath.

Involuntarily, Pandy squeezed Ghida's arm, watching as every muscle in Atlas's body grew taut.

With a tremendous yell, Atlas, in one slow motion, lifted the entire vault of the heavens onto his back. As he straightened his legs, his body growing another several meters, there were horrifying cracks heard echoing off the farthest mountains as the heavens were lifted out of their unnatural bends and curves and raised back into the smooth dome that covered the earth. Those who had already reached the rim of the mountain trying to escape began to shriek as, before their eyes, the black void that circled Jbel

Toubkal and its brother mountains began to lift and expose the terrain below.

In only a few seconds, men on the columns, those who had not fainted, were yelling joyously, begging to be let down.

"Cover your eyes," Pandy said to Ghida, Ismailil, and Amri as the heavens settled into place overhead.

"Why?" Ismailil asked.

"Wait for it," Pandy answered, throwing her arm over her eyes for good measure.

"Do it," Ghida said, her eyes closed tight.

Both boys snapped their lids shut just as the sunlight, with nothing to obscure it, hit the village in full force. Many people, their eyes accustomed only to dim, filtered light, gasped in pain.

"When can we open them?" Amri asked.

"Just give it a second and open them slowly," Pandy answered. Moments later, they were blinking at each other. Looking down, Pandy saw people of every size and color jumping with glee, knocking down columns, wriggling and prying their way out of shackles, and running to embrace each other. Without warning, Ghida threw her arms around Pandy.

Pandy hugged her tightly, turning her head a bit to gaze up at her uncle.

His eyes were shut and there was no movement

behind them, only a deep furrow in his brow and a measured breathing through gritted teeth.

"That's why he looked around so long before he lifted," Pandy thought, her heart suddenly aching for her uncle. "For his memory. The heavens are so heavy, he can't even open his eyes."

"Hey!" came a shout from below. "Either you come down or we're gonna come up!"

Pandy broke from Ghida and looked over the edge. Alcie was standing with her hands on her hips. Homer was shielding both her and Iole from the crush of people hurrying to collect their things before racing off the mountain.

"You're free!" Pandy cried.

"Homer's got his strength back!" Alcie yelled. "Hurry up, before people start stealing our stuff!"

"Keep your cloak on." Pandy grinned. "We're coming."

When they were all on the ground, Pandy found herself in the middle of a large group hug. Without warning, she found herself sobbing uncontrollably onto Alcie's shoulder.

"Hey . . . hey. Tangerines," Alcie said softly, looking Pandy right in the eye. "You did good."

"Yeah. Yeah. We all did." Pandy snuffled, smiling.

CHAPTER TWENTY-EIGHT
On the Road

For two days they walked the road through the mountains with thousands of other ex-slaves now journeying homeward; two days of talking freely, telling stories, making occasional stops for Homer (although his strength and stamina were replenishing by the hour), sharing provisions, and not a little laughter.

Sitting around a great fire on the second night, fighting back tears as she thought of how much Dido loved the warmth of her fire grate back home, hoping that Hera was keeping him warm, fed, and not leashed with a chain or a rope, Pandy suddenly remembered the magic rope still embedded in Amri's leg. As Alcie held everyone captive, recounting for the umpteenth time how Hephaestus had impulsively hugged her in the *Syracusa*'s armory, telling her she was his favorite, Pandy pulled out her wolfskin diary.

"Watch this," she said, handing it to Ismailil and Amri. "Dear diary . . ."

At once, the eyes began to glow and the large ears pricked up.

"Good evening, Pandora. Long time no talk. What have you to tell?" the diary began, then it saw the gaping faces of Ismailil and Amri. "Oh! Hello, um, and who are you two?"

"Diary," said Pandy, "please recount for us the day I turned thirteen and what Sabina made for my special evening meal."

"My pleasure," said the diary. "Oh, the horrors . . ."

As the two little boys listened closely, Pandy muttered under her breath.

"Rope, come to me."

Instantly, she saw a faint rippling under the skin of Amri's leg. Amri idly scratched at it but continued listening to the diary. There was a small movement in the dirt between Pandy and the boys, then suddenly the rope, no thicker than a hair, was coiled in her palm.

"A little thicker."

The rope expanded to a nice portable size, and Pandy tucked it into her pouch. Then she realized there was something else that needed doing, something much more important.

Later that night, as everyone else slept comfortably

around the dying embers (Alcie snoring peacefully with her head on Homer's chest), Pandy and Iole transferred Misery into the larger box. They didn't dare let the tiny woman out, but it was Iole's assumption that the smaller box could simply go in whole, adamant shackles and all.

"Gods," Pandy said, "you're right about everything else, let's hope you're right about this. One, two . . . three!"

They flipped the clasp, opened the lid of the box, and slid the smaller box inside. Pandy felt a jolt of fear as the lid refused to close for a split second, then easily settled into place as the smaller box fizzled away inside.

"I don't care what he looks like or who his favorite is," Iole said. "Hephaestus is supremely . . . cool."

"What are you two little satyrs whispering about back there?" Alcie asked, turning around.

"Nothing," said Amri.

"Nothing, my big piece of orange rind! Spill it," Alcie said, falling back to jostle the little boy playfully.

They had come to another fork leading to yet another distant mountain. At each of the previous forks, Ghida had stopped to question ex-slaves on the whereabouts of her husband. One woman had told her he'd last been seen working at a mixing pit on the mountain that now lay directly to their left. Moving off the main road, Ghida looked at Pandy, Iole, and Homer. She looked at Alcie roughhousing with her sons, knowing they all must part and not knowing what to say.

"We were just thinking that maybe Pandy could come live with us," Ismailil said, grinning and looking at the ground.

"Pandy?" Alcie cried, tickling Ismailil. "What about me, huh? What am I, chopped chimera?"

"Okay, okay . . . you can come, too!" Ismailil fell over laughing.

"Boys, hush!" Ghida said at last. "It's time to say farewell."

"No!" Amri grabbed ahold of Pandy's hand and Homer's cloak.

"Hush now!" Ghida said softly.

"You're sure you want to go up there?" Pandy asked.

"If my husband is alive, I will find him. I believe he is," Ghida said, and pointed to her heart. "In here."

"We know the feeling," Iole said.

Alcie, Iole, and Homer gave the boys tight hugs, then Pandy knelt down and spoke to them both.

"Okay, guys, be good and help your mother," she said.

" 'Kay," said Ismailil.

"Will you come back?" asked Amri.

"I don't think I—"

"Will we ever see you again?" asked Ismailil, his lower lip quivering.

Pandy thought a moment.

"Yep. You'll see me again," she said.

"Promise?" asked Amri.

"Promise. I don't know when, but somehow . . . I'll do it."

"Oh! Oh!" Amri suddenly squealed. "Ismailil tell her! Oh! We saw something, Pandy. Remember, Ismailil? The old man had the same thing . . . it was just like yours, Pandy."

Suddenly a pinecone hit Pandy right between the eyes.

"Ow!"

"Mother, look!" cried Amri, instantly distracted.

Everyone turned to see nearly a hundred gray squirrels covering a patch of nearby rocks, with the largest of them standing on his haunches in the center, another pinecone in his little claw.

"That's Dionysus's attack squirrel?" Iole asked.

"Duh!" said Pandy.

All at once, the troop of squirrels gave Pandy a right-paw salute and began moving in formation alongside the path that Ghida was about to take. Pandy smiled.

"Guess what, guys? I think you're going to have an escort! Maybe they'll help you find food and keep you warm at night."

"The furry blanket?" Ismailil asked.

"Maybe . . . hope so. Better hurry!" Pandy said, standing up.

"Good-bye, Pandora," Ghida said. "Thank you for taking care of my children. All of you . . . thank you."

"Good-bye," Pandy replied with a last hug.

Pandy and her friends watched the trio head toward the mountain, waving until they were almost out of sight, then moved again into the line of traffic.

As night fell, Pandy realized that she recognized the particular stretch of road they were on as having been the exact spot where she and the boys had been captured. No shackles and no crawling meant they were now making decent time, but Pandy was still anxious.

"How much more walking until we reach the sea?" Alcie said, almost reading Pandy's mind.

"We should reach the shore in two weeks," said Homer quietly. "There's nothing to slow us down."

"Oh, Homie, you're doing so well," Alcie said sweetly, massaging his fingers. "You're sure you're not feeling any aftereffects?"

"I don't know why not, but, like, no," he said.

"Tuh-riffic!" Alcie said.

"So, where are we going next?" Iole asked after a moment.

"Yeah, 'bout time to find out." Pandy sighed, taking the bowl map out of her pouch.

Two minutes later, after adding a few tears from her glass vial and waiting for the rings on the outside of the bowl to finally align, Pandy held the bowl aloft for all to see the brightly lit symbols.

"Mount Pelion," said Iole. "That's in Thessaly."

"Lust," said Alcie.

"And we have 129 days left," said Pandy.

Two weeks later to the day, they all crested the same brown sand dune where Alcie, Iole, and Homer had been taken prisoner weeks before. Dozens of ships were either being loaded as they lay beached or waiting out in the water for their turn to pull in.

"What the—?" cried Alcie. "How did they know?"

"I surmise that when the heavens were restored to their proper place," Iole said, "wealthier families, cities, and countries probably sent ships to carry their citizens back home."

As they stared at the gangplanks and rope ladders teeming with people, they knew it was true.

"All aboard for Syria! Syria this way," shouted one sailor, directing passengers.

"Decapolis by way of Samaria!"

"Asia Minor! Departing in five minutes for Asia Minor!"

"Germania Magna with one layover in Macedonia, right here!"

"Boarding now for Caphareus, Scyros, Thessaly, Samothrace, and points north!"

"That's us," said Pandy, looking at the massive ship a short way down the beach. "Let's go."

But as they walked up the rickety wooden gangplank, Pandy heard another cry farther down.

"Crete, Delos, and Athens! Crete, Delos, and Athens! All aboard for Southern Greece! Board!"

Pandy stopped, standing stock-still halfway up the gangplank, blocking Alcie, Iole, and Homer from moving forward, staring at the beautiful Grecian ship with spotless white sails. As the people behind them began to shove and shout, Pandy looked at Iole, a wave of homesickness pouring over her.

"I want to go home," she whispered to Iole, tears beginning to course down her cheeks. "I want to go *home*."

"I know," Iole whispered in return. "I know, Pandy. And we will."

She grabbed Pandy's hand and nudged her up onto the ship bound for Thessaly and Mount Pelion. Pandy stood on the deck with Iole and Alcie while Homer found them cots below and men around them made ready to put out to sea.

"You know, if we looked at the map right now, the

day counter would read 115," Pandy said softly, watching the sailors on the ship bound for Greece pulling up her ropes, her oarsmen guiding her out into the straight and the wind filling her sails.

"Plenty of time," Iole said.

"Really?" Pandy said, a touch of alarm in her voice. *"Really?"*

"Really," Iole said, slipping her arm around Pandy's waist, only to find that Alcie's arm was already there.

"We're good, Pandy," said Alcie, the three friends gazing back at the bleak land they'd just left as the ship pulled away from the shore. "We're good."

EPILOGUE . . . THE FIRST

Prometheus slumped down into the giant floor pillow, trying to avoid Hermes' eyes without actually *looking* like he was avoiding them.

"Okay, my friend," he said casually, "many thanks."

"You're welcome," said Hermes calmly, standing with his arms folded, the wings on his golden helmet once again brushing the ceiling.

"So, I'm gonna go check on Xander. See if Sabina's all right."

"Good idea."

"I don't want to, you know, keep you."

Hermes was silent.

"From whatever you might need . . . to . . . do."

"You honestly think I'm leaving?" Hermes said.

"Uh, well . . ."

"You actually think I'd leave this house without you telling me?"

"Tell you what?" Prometheus stood and tried to gaze nonchalantly out the window.

"You start getting all coy on me now, pal, and I'll turn you into an old man, *permanento*!"

"Uh . . ."

"What did you say to your brother to get him to pick up the heavens?"

"Oh, that."

"Sheesh! Okay, I know all your blather about responsibility, honor, and integrity didn't do any good, soooo . . . was it gory and bloody? Did you tell him you'd fight him until he was senseless?"

"No."

"Did you tell him that Zeus would chain him up with the rest of your family in Tartarus?"

"Not exactly."

"Hack off his arms?"

"Hermes!"

"Then *what*?"

"I just told him . . ."

"Yes?" Hermes said eagerly.

". . . that our mother, Clymene . . ."

"Yes, yes?"

". . . and Atlas was always her favorite, mind you . . ."

"Yes, right . . ."

". . . would be very disappointed in him, and . . ."

"And?"

". . . wouldn't like him best anymore."

Hermes' jaw fell open. After a good minute in which the two friends just stared at each other, Hermes started laughing first, followed by Prometheus. The two quickly became hysterical.

"Okay, okay . . . the best part?" Prometheus choked.

"Lay it on me!"

"The part about our mother?"

"Yeah?"

"It's true! He's her favorite!"

"Oh, stop . . . stop!"

The two were laughing so hard Hermes thought he'd pulled a muscle somewhere and Prometheus collapsed over his wooden table.

"Oh, you Titans!" Hermes wheezed. "Man! Your whole family is a trip!"

EPILOGUE . . . THE SECOND

Hera lumbered along the path through the beautiful garden that led to Aeolus's workshop, the swinging folds of her blue robes knocking the blooms off of rare roses, irises, and lilies. As she turned a corner quickly, her right sleeve took out a whole row of stunning white hydrangeas.

She didn't even notice.

She approached the massive wooden door and walked right through it without so much as a knock.

"Okay, here's the deal," she called furiously to the lone, white-haired figure staring out the enormous windows on the opposite side of the room. "This time I need a wind that will—"

"Will what, dearest?" said the figure, turning.

Hera stopped dead in her tracks.

"*Zeus!* I mean . . . Zeus. Husband. Love of my life . . . why are you . . . ?"

"Here, my dovelet?"

"Yes, light of my mornings. And why dressed like that?"

Zeus, indeed, sported a strange, short sleeveless garment over his toga, which seemed to have many pouches on the outside. The pouches were stuffed with small metal hooks of varying shapes and tiny fish, causing an unpleasant odor. He also held two long poles, each with an even longer string of leather attached to one end.

"You see, my precious little calf, I have decided to take a small vacation, and who better to bring along on my holiday than my dear friend Aeolus?"

At that moment, Aeolus stepped into the workroom, dressed almost exactly like Zeus, carrying two straw hats and an oversized wineskin.

"Now this should work . . . I filled the outer skin with ice so the wine should stay nice and cold."

He saw Hera standing by the worktables.

"Ohhh, hi." His voice dropped almost two octaves.

"Aeolus," Hera greeted him coolly.

"Ah, good! A hat! Pardon me, my dangerously overfed lamby-kins," Zeus said, stepping around Hera, taking a hat from Aeolus, and cocking it jauntily on his head. "And here is your pole, my friend, and . . . well, I think that's it, isn't it? Oh, except Hera wanted something of you . . . what was it, darling one? Oh, yes . . . a wind!

You wanted a wind. Well, you came to the right place. What kind of wind and why?"

Hera's lips wiggled slightly, her teeth gnashing together in her mouth as she fought to think of something to say.

"I just found a lovely perfume from Thrace . . . yes, Thrace, and . . . and I want a gentle wind constantly about my neck to blow it about and please those around me."

"Well, my enormous oatie-cake, much as I would love to put something around your neck, your request doesn't sound too urgent and I'm sure it can wait until our return. Don't you agree?"

"Yes, my one and only love," Hera said, low.

"Excellent!" Zeus cried, ushering Aeolus out the big wooden workroom door. "Coming, my tall, frothy glass of nectar?"

Hera hurried to catch up to the two immortals already waiting on the path outside.

"Ooops, almost forgot . . . don't want to tempt thieves," Zeus said. With a blink of his eye, a giant bar of adamant slid into place neatly across the door, barring entrance from the outside.

"Loved one," Zeus said, kissing his wife on her cheek, "I shall see you when I see you. Have fun and try not to get into trouble. Love you! Aeolus, come!"

Without so much as a backward glance at Hera, Zeus and Aeolus strode away down the path.

It was only when Hera, in a state of utter confusion and defeat, turned to check the door did she see the sign: blue indigo ink on a large piece of white parchment.

GONE FISHING!

EPILOGUE . . . THE THIRD

"You're sure you don't want us to wait here? We'd be happy to, you know."

"No. Thanks, but I'll be fine."

Prometheus turned away from Bellerophon and stared past Pegasus, who was sticking his pink nose into a cold oven, and out over the ruins of the village on top of Jbel Toubkal.

"Go fly around for a bit, get Pegasus some oats, find a pretty girl to chat up."

"Highly unlikely around here. When do you want us back?" Bellerophon asked.

"Well, he deserves some answers," Prometheus said, nodding to Atlas in the distance behind them. "There's a lot he needs to know. And I have to proceed delicately. I'd give it a couple of hours."

"Right. We'll be back in two."

"Thanks again for the lift, my friend," Prometheus said.

"No problem. It was a slow day anyway, right Pegasus?" Bellerophon called.

Pegasus nodded his head in assent and half flew, half pranced over to his master. Bellerophon quickly grabbed the jewel-encrusted bridle and swung himself up onto the horse's back, ever mindful not to bump his wings.

"See you!" Bellerophon said.

"See you," Prometheus replied, giving Pegasus a quick pat on the cheek before the horse shot into the sky and over the rim of the mountain.

Prometheus picked his way over the immense amount of rubble. The freed slaves had destroyed nearly everything in a raging, violent exodus from the village. Finally, he stood at his brother's feet.

"Hey, Brother!" he called. "It's me, Prometheus. I'm coming up. Don't get nervous when I start talking in your ear. I am not a nesting bird. Do not swat me! I repeat, *do not swat me!*"

With the tip of his finger, Prometheus began to heat the air directly under his backside. Slowly, as the air became lighter, Prometheus began to rise on an invisible, superheated column.

"Getting closer," he called to Atlas, halfway up.

"Almost there . . . almost . . . and . . ." He leveled off right next to his brother's ear. "Hi."

Atlas let out a huge breath through his teeth.

"Okay, I'll talk, you just listen," Prometheus said.

Atlas gave the tiniest grunt imaginable.

"First of all, Mom wants me to tell you that she loves you and is very proud of you. She understands . . . we all do . . . that you had absolutely no control over your actions and are truly blameless. Okay? Okay. Now . . ."

Prometheus took a deep breath, suddenly realizing he didn't know where to start. He focused on reheating the column of air while he tried to find the right words.

"So . . . so you're probably wondering what in Hades has been happening around here for the past few weeks, right? Right. Well, Brother, it actually all started a while back, with your niece, Pandora. Pandy, she likes to be called. And you've met her already. You . . . you just didn't know it was her at the time. Okay, let me go back to the beginning. So, you remember my theft of fire and the big eagle that ate my liver? Well, there was also this box . . . and . . . and now there's a quest . . ."

Prometheus began to laugh in spite of himself. He gazed out, past the rim of the mountain, toward the sun just beginning to slide down to the horizon.

"Oh, dear Brother, wait till I tell you about my girl!"

GLOSSARY

Names, pronunciations, and descriptions of gods, demigods, other integral immortals, places, objects, and fictional personages appearing within these pages. Definitions derived from three primary sources: Edith Hamilton's *Mythology: Timeless Tales of Gods and Heroes*; Webster's Online Dictionary, which derives many of its definitions from Wikipedia, the free encyclopedia (further sources are also indicated on this Web site); and the author's own brain.

Atlas (AT-lass): one of the original Titans and, in some myths, Prometheus's brother. Zeus condemned Atlas to bear the crushing vault of the heavens on his shoulders forever. (Often he is portrayed as also having to hold up the earth as well, but that's just illogical. I mean, think about it, where would he stand? Hmm?)

Balearic Islands (buh-LAIR-ick): a group of islands in the western Mediterranean Sea, off the coast of Spain.

Espania (ess-PAN-ia): an archaic (or ancient) name for Spain.

fenugreek (FEN-you-greek): annual herb of southern Europe and eastern Asia having off-white flowers and aromatic seeds used medicinally and in curry.

Hiero II (HERO): ruler (and tyrant) of Syracuse from 270 to 215 BC.

Jbel Toubkal (juh-BELL toob-CALL . . . but say it fast!): sometimes written as Jebel Toubkal. At 4,167 meters, it is the highest peak in the Atlas Mountains and in North Africa.

Mauretania (more-ih-TAIN-ia): a Roman province on the Mediterranean coast of North Africa, where Algeria is now, east of Morocco.

parasite (PAR-uh-site): an animal or plant that lives in or on a host (another animal or plant); the parasite obtains nourishment from the host without benefiting or killing the host.

Somnus (SOM-nuss): the Roman God of Sleep. The Greek name for the same god is Hypnus.

Styx (STICKS): a river in Hades across which Charon carried dead souls.

Ulmus rubra (UHL-muss ROOB-ruh): an elm with a hard wood inner bark that can be ground into a nutrient-rich paste. The bark also contains a mucilage that is used as a remedy for sore throats and in poultices.

ACKNOWLEDGMENTS

Thank you to Harriet Shapiro, PhD; Marcia Wallace; Scott Hennesy; Antoinette Spolar-Levine; Phyllis Kramer; Deb Shapiro; Tom Stacey; Rosemary Rossi; Simon Lewis; Debby O'Connor; Michy and the Cool-ettes; and Dominic Friesen.

Special thanks to Elizabeth Schonhorst, Caroline Abbey, Minnie, Josie, Rosie, and Sara.

DONALD AGNELLI

Carolyn Hennesy

is also the author of *Pandora Gets Jealous*, *Pandora Gets Vain*, and *Pandora Gets Heart*. A Los Angeles native, she has more than twenty-five years' experience in the entertainment industry and can currently be seen on the daytime drama *General Hospital*. In addition to her full-time acting and writing careers, Ms. Hennesy also teaches improvisational comedy and has become a flying-trapeze artist. She lives in the Los Angeles area with her fab husband, cool cat, and groovy dog.

www.pandyinc.com
www.carolynhennesy.com

READ ON FOR A SNEAK PEEK AT
PANDORA'S NEXT MYTHIC MISADVENTURE

PANDORA
Gets Heart

Carolyn Hennesy

"Everyone up!" Eteocles was shouting the next morning. Pandy woke with a start. She'd been dreaming that Athena was offering her some ambrosia and nectar, saying, "Come on! Become immortal . . . you know you want to!" Suddenly waking up, surrounded by tall trees, she had no idea where she was. Alcie's palm accidentally mashed down on Pandy's wrist as Alcie lifted herself off the tarp.

"Ow!" Pandy said, and instantly she remembered that she was somewhere on Mount Pelion, looking for Lust.

"Sorry," Alcie said, jumping down off the cart.

Once more, after a hasty first meal of creamed oats ("Where did he get oats?" Pandy had whispered to Iole. "I always keep a spare pouch handy," Eteocles had called out), they were off again. Alcie stubbed her toe, then Iole twisted her ankle, then Pandy tripped getting the cart out of a hole and landed on her face; she was getting more and more frustrated. But they had only walked for a few hours when Eteocles brought the oxen to a halt.

"Very well," Eteocles began.

"Is this where you drop us off and get that hour's head start?" Pandy asked snidely.

Even Alcie looked at her.

"Touchy this morning, aren't we?" Eteocles replied.

"We've walked for, basically, two days," Pandy said, her anger rising. "We could have done that ourselves."

"You wouldn't have known where to go if you'd been by yourselves," Eteocles answered, his voice calm.

"We'd have gotten here," Alcie said.

"We actually helped you get this cart up the mountain. We don't mind paying, but not for something unfair. You need to give back the bracelet," Pandy said firmly.

Eteocles paused for a second, then threw back his head and laughed. Pandy saw a strange, thin pale line zigzag down his face. Then another. All at once, he began to grow. As he became larger and larger, his wrinkled brown skin began to crack, peel away, and drop to the ground, revealing taut, perfect white skin covering bulging muscles. The dirty toga was transformed into a clean, bright, silvery fabric, and the grayish hair became golden and curly, topped with a beautiful winged helmet.

"Down!" Pandy cried to the other three, who were staring, stupefied.

Instantly, all four were on their knees, heads bowed.

"Pears! Is that who I think it is?" Alcie whispered.

"Yes! Shhhh!" Pandy hissed back.

After a second of silence, she lifted her eyes.

"Okay, missy," Hermes said with a grin, his arms

folded across his massive chest, staring straight at her. "You are getting *spunky*!"

"I'm so sorry," Pandy began.

"What's with the 'sorry'?" Hermes said. "I like it! All right . . . everybody up!"

Instantly, Pandy and the rest were on their feet.

"Eyes on me."

Everyone looked straight at Hermes.

"Try not to look terrified," Hermes said to the group as he walked toward Alcie.

"Hello, Alcestis," he said softly, and then turned to the others. "Oh, I just realized . . . Pandora is the only one who's actually met me. And yet I feel like I know all of you so well."

"Mighty Hermes, swift and fleet footed," Alcie began.

"Yes, Alcestis, thank you. I know," Hermes said. "You're doing very nice work."

"Uh, thanks," Alcie said.

"Homer," Hermes said, approaching the youth. "Now, aren't you glad you didn't try to flatten me? It would have gotten out of hand . . . probably a little ugly. But you kept your cool and, hey, good times!"

"Uh . . ."

"I like you, Homer. We all do. Not the brightest lamp in the temple, but you have heart. And a noble soul."

"Yes. Thank you. I think," Homer said.

"Well, you try to and that's what matters. Hello, Iole."

"Wondrous Hermes . . ."

"Ach, can't anyone just say 'hello'?" Hermes rolled his eyes. "Okay, enough! Now, instructions first, questions afterward. I could be all godlike and get a little flowery but that would get us nowhere fast, and since you all need to get somewhere fast, I'll put it to you straight. You're going back in time. All of you. Many centuries. What you seek has traveled the river of ages—sorry, that was flowery. I'm going to get you there and bring you back, that's if you're all still alive. Here's the rule: don't change anything in the past or it will alter the future. Seriously. And it might not be good. Any questions?"

"Uh, yes," Iole said, thinking fast, as the others just looked at one another, confused. "How far back are we going?"

"Roughly thirteen centuries. Next?"

"Lust is . . . is . . . back in time?" Pandy asked.

"Alcie, what's the word you always say when somebody says something obvious? Starts with a delta, I think," Hermes asked.

"Uh, 'duh'?"

"That's it! Duh!"

"Are you going to stay with us?" Pandy asked.

"Let me put it this way. I'll be there, and I'll know you're you, but don't look to me for help of any kind until and only if you're ready to come back."

"Oh!" gasped Iole suddenly.

Hermes stared at her for a second.

"You have it, don't you?" he asked.

"Mount Pelion . . . thirteen hundred years ago," she started.

"Give or take," Hermes said casually.

"Oh! Oh! And they're *all* going to be here?"

"What? Who!" Alcie cried, whacking Iole on her arm.

"Almost all," said Hermes, smiling. "Someone's missing. But then, you knew that, didn't you?"

"Iole?" Pandy said, looking at her quizzically.

"Enough gab," Hermes said. "Time's a'wasting, and how. Everybody grab a little piece of my toga—don't get fresh—and we'll be off."

Pandy, Alcie, Iole, and Homer each pinched a small amount of the silver fabric and instinctively braced themselves for a whirlwind journey back through time. Alcie and Iole hunched over as if preparing to face a horrible hurricane. Pandy clutched her pouch to her chest and planted her feet firmly on the ground. Homer grabbed his cloak with his free hand and closed his eyes, head down.

"Alcie, Iole . . . what are you doing?" Hermes asked.

"We're hanging on. Won't there be wind . . . or something?" Alcie yelled.

Pandy, looking at her toes, saw a small shift, a subtle repositioning of the stones on the ground around her feet. She noticed that the birds that had been singing were silenced, and a small white boulder had materialized on a patch of grass off to her left . . . and then nothing.

"You four are crazy!" Hermes laughed. "You look like you're about to be attacked! It's done. We're there."

"That's it?" Pandy asked, looking around.

"That's it," Hermes said.

"I just thought there would be . . . wind," Alcie said, standing up straight.

"You're . . . ," Pandy began.

"I'm what? Fabulous?" Hermes asked.

"No. I mean, yes! But you're *helping*." Pandy's voice dropped to a whisper on the last word.

"I did, and I might again," Hermes said. "Now don't blow it by asking a lot of questions."

The forest surrounding them was essentially the same. Some trees were taller, some were smaller, and some were new. There was a different cloud formation in the sky, but there was no other marked visible difference.

"I'm off," Hermes said, then pointed east. "Your way lies down that road. Remember, change nothing."

He stepped back and Pandy thought he was about to disappear when he stopped and turned to Iole.

"You're kidding, right?"

Iole's mouth fell open and then she looked down at the ground.

"I'm sorry."

"At a time like this, *that's* what you're thinking about?" Hermes asked. I would have expected that of Alcie, not you."

"Huh?" Alcie said.

"I'm sorry," Iole said again.

"A deal is a deal, Iole. It doesn't matter that I probably can't use it. So, no, you can't have the bracelet back."

Iole nodded.

Hermes shook his head and disappeared in a bright white flash.

"Nice going, Miss I-Can-Give-Away-My-Presents," Alcie said after a pause. "Now he hates us!"

"No he doesn't, Alcie. Quit it," Pandy said. "Iole, what in Zeus's name is going on? What do you know?"

"Did either of you *ever* pay attention when Master Epeus was teaching ancient Greek history? *Ever?* Thirteen hundred years ago, Zeus was in love with the goddess Thetis. Hera found out about it and got so angry that not only did she force Zeus to stop seeing Thetis, she made Zeus give Thetis to a mortal man as his wife."

"Oh, yeah! I was awake for this," Pandy cried. "King Peleus! Whose palace is . . . was . . . is on Mount Pelion!"

"Correct!" Iole continued. "It was a huge celebration to which all the gods and goddesses were invited."

"Except one," Pandy said.

"Correct again. And if my guess is right, today is the big—"

"Do you think you have been hired to simply stand around!"

A shrill voice, like the sound of a horn, high and off-key, pierced the quiet of the forest. Pandy, Alcie, Iole, and Homer whipped their heads around.

Then their jaws dropped.

Read all the books in the
Tales of the Frog Princess series!

"[A] brilliantly created world of magic and mayhem." —VOYA

www.edbakerbooks.com

www.talesofedbaker.com

BLOOMSBURY